In memory of Nigel Greenwood, 1941–2004

ICE

They left the house, father and son, by the back door. The day was bright, but bitter cold. The boy was well-wrapped with a mother's eye for detail – scarf tucked into his jacket, hat over his ears, mittens. On the man everything was adrift. He carried a fishing bag over his shoulder and he held his son by the elbow as if his life depended on it.

The man walked fast and his boots rang out. The boy ran beside him like a hobbled colt. This was how they went along until they reached the church; then the man let go of his son's elbow to unlatch the gate. Through the gate and beneath the spreading yew they walked, the man less sure now, his boots quieter.

Inside the church, the man dropped his bag on a pew and put his clothes in order, buttoning and belting. The boy stood at the head of the nave and waited. He felt beneath the scarf for the chain, and ran his finger down to St Christopher, warm against his skin. His breath made little clouds. He banged his feet for warmth and the thin air swallowed up the sound. The boy tucked his arms about himself and turned around slowly. He looked at the bright eagle and the slitty-eyed men and dragons near the door. His stomach growled with hunger. He looked at the stained glass picture with Mary carrying Baby Jesus, his halo like a cushion behind his head. Underneath, the boy made out the names of Robert and William and the date,

1918, which was before he was born.

'So —,' the man said. 'Ready?'

'I'm hungry,' the boy said. 'Can we have breakfast now?'

They sat in a pew and the boy chewed some bread.

'Look.' The man showed the boy four squares of chocolate. 'I saved it.'

'For our adventure,' the boy said.

They walked across the flat graves to the kissing gate in the corner of the churchyard. The father went through first, then the son. They walked down beside the first beet field, and the second. The boy stepped on the hummocks when he could; but sometimes he couldn't and the snow was deeper in between, and it made his socks wet above his boots.

'This is too deep for Meg,' the boy said. 'She'd need carrying.'

At the end of the second beet field they were into the woods. The snow was heavier and wetter here, so the boy trod in his father's footsteps, jumping a little to get from one to the next.

'D'you think there'll be a cake when we get there?' he said.

The woods were quiet except for the slops of snow that fell from the branches. The sun made streaks through the trees.

'And will Aunt Ada be standing with the lantern? Like she did at Christmas?'

'We'll get there before dark if this weather holds. But Ada doesn't know about us coming, so there likely won't be cake.'

~

They walked on through the woods, father in front and son behind, the father sometimes stopping for his son to catch up, a finger drumming on his thigh.

The boy watched his feet in the snow. He'd found a stick for balancing. He didn't want to fall over again. They were making a trail through the woods, like the animals. If somebody hunted for them, they'd follow the trail and find them easily. Unless it snowed again, or melted.

'The bigger boys come here,' he said.

'We'll be going further than them,' his father said. 'It's a long way.'

'It doesn't matter if they can see where we've been on the adventure, because we're not escaping,' he said.

His father didn't reply.

'Is it the time I'd be going to school?'

His father checked his watch.

'About that.'

'And you'd be at your work.' The boy swiped his stick at a branch to see the snow fall. 'You'd be making a table, or a cabinet, or a chair.'

'I'll have no trouble,' the father said to himself. 'Ada said there's plenty of work in the city.'

'Did you tell Fred?' the boy said. 'Did he want to come too? Or he might be tracking us.'

'Stop that with the stick,' his father said. 'You're slowing us.'

They came to the edge of the trees. It was bright on the snow and they blinked in the glare. Beyond the fence the white stretched away to the horizon.

'It's like a big sea,' the boy said.

'There's a bridge down the far side, then the road,' said the man. 'We might get a ride after that, if we're lucky.'

The man set off wading the sea. He took sweeping strides to clear as much of the snow as he could for his small son. The boy stood and beat his stick at the snow.

'Meg can't walk to school without me,' he said.

'We'll be there right before dark if we can get a lift,' the man called back. 'Before the snow starts up again,' he added to himself.

'She's too small,' the boy said. He looked down at his boots, sodden with snow. It was cold, just standing.

'Come on, Will.'

'But Ma can't take her, so then Mrs Pierce will punish her.'

His father stopped and turned.

'Meg's fine,' he said, 'and you're fine. But we've to keep moving.'

'She can't go across the big road on her own,' the boy said quietly.

He stepped out into the sea, a wide, playground step, arms out for balance, then his stick planted.

'I'll show her about going over the snow. How you have to have your arms out, and not to stand still too long if your boots are wet.'

~

They walked in the middle of the road where the snow was at its firmest. The boy watched his father's boots. He was weary: his legs ached and his feet and hands were cold. He counted steps and told himself they would stop after ten, then after twenty, then on till he forgot the number he had reached and began again. It was quiet, not even the black birds rawing in the empty trees. He heard an engine sound and far down the road, at least ninety steps away, a lorry came towards them, lumbering and high. The boy looked up, two bright spots in his cold cheeks.

'It might be going back home,' he said. 'We could wave and stop it.'

His father moved to the edge of the road. The sun shone hard and the light beat up in pulses.

'We could ride on the lorry,' the boy said, 'and I could tell Ma about our adventure.'

The lorry roared up and the driver raised his hand; then it was gone.

They stopped just after and the man hoisted the boy to the top bar of a gate and brought a couple of apples out of his bag, wizened and liver-spotted. He gave them to the boy, one after the other; for himself he took a plug of tobacco from his pouch that he chewed and spat, chewed and spat onto the white snow, all the while pacing a line from the gate to the road and back. The boy ate the apples down to the shrivelled pips, splitting them between his teeth for the taste of almond.

When he had finished, his father stopped pacing and turned to him. His face was a furious colour and he spoke in a rush.

'We're not going home,' he said.

The boy licked the last of almond from his lip.

'Ada's is just for now. We'll stay with her tomorrow, then I'm going to the city. Once I've got work and some digs, I'll come back for you. We'll find a school; you'll get new friends.'

The man paused. The boy was sitting very still. Finally he looked down at his lap, then up at his father.

'We've got a house, and I've got a school, and friends.'

'So they'll be different, is all.'

'But I have to walk with Meg. And Ma needs me to fetch in the water.'

'We're not going home.'

The boy poked at the snow on the gate top, drilled a hole down to the wood with a finger.

'I don't want to go to Ada's any more, or the city. And anyhow my legs are hurting.'

'Oh, for God's sake . . .' The man flung his bag at the silent snow and walked away; then he stopped and turned.

'We can't stay here, Will,' he said in a gentle voice. 'We'll freeze before the night's done. We'll get to Ada's and then...'

'Ma doesn't know where I am. Nor Meg.'

'Your ma does know where you are.'

The boy shook his head, just a small movement, and then more fiercely, side to side.

'No,' he said. 'She doesn't.'

'She knows you're with me,' his father said.

'No,' the boy said. 'She wouldn't have let me.'

His father walked back towards him and the boy stared past him. Then he turned away, swung his legs over the gate and dropped into the field. The snow lay deep in the furrows; he sank down to his thighs. But the ridges were blown clear, and he scrambled up and ran free and high along the iron earth. He ran fast, as if his tiredness and the heavy land had let him go. By the time his father had climbed the gate, the boy was half way to the trees that lined the near side. By the time his father reached the trees, his son had disappeared between them.

'Will!' the man shouted. 'Come back!' But the snow swallowed the sound and he ran on into silence.

Will ran through the trees and over the shadows till he came to a place like a smooth, round field where the trees stopped and the sun made the snow shine. He stood still and listened. Pulling off his mittens, he picked up a handful of snow, cupped it in his palm. It turned to ice and dripped into his cuff. He sipped at it, wincing at the cold and listened again. From somewhere in the trees there was the crack of a branch breaking. Will dropped the snow, his body still as an animal's. A moment later there was the packed thud of someone running.

'I'm going home,' Will said to himself and he was off, onto the field. The ground was so flat, so clear, it was like running downhill. Animals had been across before him. There were rabbits' prints, and birds, and the cloven prints of deer. Will laughed, a whoop of sound, and kicked up his knees, faster and faster, till he was nearly in the middle and he had the sun on his shoulders.

'Will!' It was a shout. He glanced back. His father was bent forward, his bag thrown off his shoulder, one hand against a tree trunk for support.

'Stop!' His father's voice was hoarse. 'Stop. It's dangerous.'

The boy slowed to a walk, then turned to face his father across the flat snow.

'I'm going home,' he called.

'Will, you're on ice,' his father said, his voice high, pleading.

Will shook his head and walked backwards, one hand to his neck to touch St Christopher. He walked away from his father, surely, steadily, with the bearing of a child who knows what he will do.

His father stood straight, still breathing heavily, and walked to the edge. He spoke between breaths, keeping his voice lower now, calmer.

'Please. It's not safe. You could fall through.'

The boy waved and he made a little jig.

'No!' his father roared. He raised his arm. 'Wait there. Don't move.'

But seeing his father come towards him, the boy turned and ran again into the heart of the sun.

WATER

Meg sat upright in the tender and looked straight ahead. The waves were choppy and the boat bucked a little, so she had one hand on the seat to steady herself. With the other she made sure of her hat. Although the air had been dry when she arrived at the docks, out on the water there was a fine mist blowing in from the sea; by the time they reached the ship, you could be forgiven for mistaking the fret on her face for tears.

Although she didn't know it yet, she was the youngest passenger to join the upper deck, and amongst those dozen or so watching her come on board, there was much speculation as to why she was travelling at this time.

From the lower deck, a crowd of soldiers watched her too. They were the same age, just boys, their fatigues still stiff and their hair newly shorn, and they were on their way to war. The wind jostled her and caught at her skirt. Somebody wolf-whistled.

She didn't look at the soldiers, not even a glance. Held herself back from it. They probably thought she was stuck-up. She was the final passenger and as she stepped through the rail, people nodded a greeting and several introduced themselves.

Even before the steward had shown her to her cabin, the ship had weighed anchor and was on its way.

Once her trunk had been delivered, Meg locked the door, slipped off her shoes and lay down on the lower bunk. She couldn't feel the ship move, but her stomach swung as though she were on a fairground ride. Turning her head into the pillow, she shut her eyes. She was tired but the pillow smelt unfamiliar and she knew she wouldn't sleep. Her stomach rumbled. There was a chunk of cake packed away in her trunk – her mother had wrapped it up in oiled paper – but it was for her wedding day; she shouldn't eat it.

Leaving had been easier than she'd anticipated. Alice had cried every day for the last week and Joyce said that nothing would ever be the same, but Meg had felt detached, she didn't know why. She had their friendship tokens in her trunk. Mr and Mrs Gilmer had asked Meg and her mother to tea on her last Saturday. Meg had gone alone, of course, and they had fed her fit to burst and sent her home with a big cheese, sewn tight into its cloth. It would feed her mother for months.

Mrs Gilmer had cried, tears dripping onto the cheese, and told Meg she was like a daughter. Mr Gilmer told her she had the best milking hands in the county and she'd be sorely missed.

Meg was happy not to walk there in the dark each morning, her body still asleep and the wind coming off the fields so bitterly. But she would miss butting her head against the cows' warm pelts, and the clean, sharp sound of the milk hitting the bucket. And she would miss their smell.

At four o'clock she checked her face in the mirror. Tea was served in the lounge in cups and saucers of fine china and with plates of Rich Tea biscuits. There were perhaps thirty passengers drinking tea, though not many of them were women.

Meg stood at one side and looked from face to face. People smiled and nodded. The war was on, but this ship was sailing to somewhere else. Perhaps that was why they smiled. She turned to watch the thin line of England through the window, feeling better for the biscuits.

A young woman came over and introduced herself. She wore a wedding ring and was maybe five or six years older.

'Margery Richardson. You nearly didn't make it.'

'Meg Bryan,' she said.

'Travelling alone in the war. How bold.'

'My fiancé is meeting me off the boat,' Meg said.

'Family in Africa?'

'Colonial service. Essential war effort work.'

'Anyway, how sensible, not to wait.'

Meg blushed. 'He said I should come. He said it was safe as houses in a convoy.'

'Always another ship to come to the rescue,' Mrs Richardson said. 'That's what they've been telling me. Accidents do happen, of course, but fingers crossed.'

'Are you travelling with your husband?' Meg said.

'We're going home. South Africa. Been in London and had enough of the Blitz. Rather have the heat and the natives than any more bombing.'

They sat down in easy chairs and Mr Richardson came over to join them. He patted his wife on the hand and looked Meg up and down, before going in search of more tea.

'I should warn you, my husband's a journalist,' said Mrs Richardson.

'Warn me?'

'Lots of questions. He does it all the time, and he does know a terrible lot. More than ever I could.'

Mr Richardson returned and the two women listened as he told them stories and important facts about the war. Meg watched Mrs Richardson and wondered how often she had heard all these before. Mr Richardson didn't ask Meg any questions. She nodded when he paused and she thought about the future. He reminded her of George and she wondered whether she would have to tend to George in the same way.

She'd met George in the town hall when she'd gone about her father, and he'd bought her a coffee afterwards. She hadn't said very much. That she lived with her mother and worked in the village. He said he was doing exams and if he passed them, he would go and work far away.

'To London, do you mean?' Meg said. 'I'd like to go to London. I'd like to go a long way away.'

On their second date George took her for tea at the Empire. He told her he was going to go to Africa, not London, if he passed his exams and he said he thought she was the wife he needed. He was going to establish himself and that meant leaving things behind. He needed a wife who understood that; who wanted that too, and he thought she was the right woman.

On their fifth date George said he loved her, and she thought he did, in a way. He said that they must have been intended for each another. He told her what to put in her trunk for Africa and he told her what to leave behind. She left behind her mother and the village and her lost brother, though George didn't tell her to. Anyway, she understood him because it wasn't really love that had got her on this ship either.

Back in her cabin she unpacked her things. She put her bible on the dressing table and stood the photograph of George next to it, beside the mirror. It had been taken in a studio before he left and he looked out solemnly with his brand-new shorts and his white knees and his highly-polished shoes. The silk camisole and knickers, still wrapped in tissue-paper, she stowed in the top drawer. Alice had given them to her as a parting gift, a little smile like a shadow.

'For your wedding night,' she'd said.

The snapshot of her mother she put beneath her pillow. Along the corridor she found the bathroom. It was clean, though it smelt odd. She washed her face in warm, salty water and when she ran the water out of the sink, the sea seemed very close, as if it might rise up in there at any minute.

'Don't be foolish,' she said to herself.

She started the letter to her mother.

Dear Ma,

All is well with me. The train journey was a little long and I was glad of your bread. It kept me going. There were fresh eggs and butter in the guesthouse. I only got lost once, getting to the docks. Now I am on board the ship which is huge, you can't imagine. There is plenty to eat, so you mustn't worry on that score. Everybody is very polite. It is

*smart as a hotel, with stewards asking if you'd like more tea,
and so forth, which is nice but a bit tiring.*

*I am sure I will get used to it in two weeks. There are
soldiers on board too, on their way to the war. I don't
imagine their quarters are like a hotel.*

It was getting dark by dinner time and a steward knocked on
Meg's door to ask her to cover the portholes properly. She
took her lifejacket with her to dinner, as instructed. Standing
in the doorway, she looked across the room. The tables were
set with starched linen, silver cutlery and several glasses at
each place. Meg had only eaten in a restaurant once before
and that was with George, the evening he proposed to her.

She was wondering where to sit, since most of the tables
were full, when Mrs Richardson waved from the far side.
George had advised her to mix on the ship because she might
become acquainted with useful people, but it was only the
first night and she was tired. If she sat with the Richardsons,
she wouldn't have to remember any more names.

There was Chicken Chasseur with rice, more than she
could eat. She hadn't seen this much chicken for years. Mr
Richardson leaned towards her with his knife and fork.

'If you're not finishing it?' he said.

She would write about Mr Richardson to her mother.

'The thing about us journalists is we've always got a story
to tell,' he said. His cheek bulged with chicken. 'Never short
of a tale, so always in demand.'

Meg didn't like Mr Richardson's manners, nor did she like

Mrs Richardson's kowtowing. But she knew they were what George called a certain sort of person and she could learn about serviettes and how to hold your knife. So she sat quietly and watched.

The war had distilled the passengers eating dinner that night into a particular kind of group. There were no frivolous travellers, though nobody was talking very much about the dangers. But every passenger had at least one good reason to risk this journey: marriage, family, money. There were no children, few women and, apart from Mr Richardson and a clergyman, all the men were over a certain age. Although they were deemed too old to fight, many nevertheless wore their years with an air of apology, stooping more than they might usually; and they were quick, that first evening, to mention former injuries, especially those received in any kind of line of duty.

'You arrived too late to see the soldiers,' said Mrs Richardson. 'They were quite a sight.'

'Really.'

'Hundreds and hundreds of them.'

'Five platoons, and some. Five hundred and forty-eight of them,' said Mr Richardson.

Mrs Richardson shook her head. 'I found it quite distressing. Funny, because I've seen enough parades in London. I think it was seeing them so close-up. They look so young and so unpractised.'

'I've watched all the boys from my village leave,' Meg said.

'No one from your family?'

'No. But I knew them all. Since we were children.'

Mr Richardson laughed. 'One of them could be on this ship . . . I could probably find out . . . My sources.'

Meg shook her head. This was too near the bone. 'They're all fighting already. But are you writing an article?'

Mr Richardson sat back, his hands across his stomach. 'I'm planning a piece about the ship. Our heroic lads, some statistics, what the ship was in peacetime. A few personal stories, like the girl willing to risk the U-boats to join her betrothed.'

He winked at Meg – 'Need a whisky' – and left the table.

'I don't want to be in a newspaper,' Meg said. 'And I'm sure George wouldn't like it,' though in truth she thought George might be delighted.

'Do your parents approve?' Mrs Richardson said.

Meg wasn't sure what she meant.

'My father is dead,' she said.

'Oh, I'm sorry.'

'It was a long time ago,' Meg said. But perhaps her face had given something away, because it was true that the shock of feeling still took her by surprise; grief and guilt, such old guilt, because maybe it was her fault he was gone; because how could she miss the man who'd made her mother so unhappy? Who'd taken her brother? And the tug she still felt in her body, not her mind: the longing for a solid feeling and a smell that was pipe smoke and shaving soap and something else she couldn't describe but that she knew was her father.

'It's very romantic. Quite an adventure,' Mrs Richardson said.

But her pa doesn't want her to go on the adventure too. He doesn't want her to go out with Will. He shouts at her, and her ma shouts at her pa because Will hasn't had any breakfast.

Her ma is crying, so Meg says shush to her. She says it in her ma's shush voice. 'Shush, ma; shush now. It's only an adventure. I'll kiss it better.'

Her ma holds something in her hand, she cries on it and she doesn't listen. So Meg goes out of the room and up the steep stairs. She climbs onto the bed and reaches with her arm under the covers. It's still warm where Will's body and hers have been. She takes off her shoes, pushes her legs back under and lies still. Her pinafore skirt is runkled and her cardigan is bunched under her back. She moves her legs this way and that, to keep all the warmth, but just her legs aren't enough, so she gets out again.

'My mother is very fond of George,' Meg said. 'She thinks him very steady.'

'Brothers and sisters?' Mrs Richardson said.

Meg had thought about this question; she had practised saying no, she didn't have any; no, she was an only child. She shook her head. 'I don't know.'

She saw Mrs Richardson's raised eyebrows, and behind her, Mr Richardson returning from the bar, and she stood up. 'I'm tired, and a bit chilly,' she said. 'Will you excuse me?'

Careful not to lose her way, Meg walked to her cabin. She wanted to be left alone; she had dreamed of it, coming on this ship. That was something she liked about George – he didn't ask her about her family because she was to leave it all behind in marrying him.

Everything in the cabin was as she had left it. Nothing had

21

been picked up and put down; nothing had been wept over. She was so glad to be by herself. She lay down to sleep and prayed she would not dream.

Over breakfast, Meg continued with her letter:

> *I am still waking at 5.30, but no cows to milk here. Just now I am eating fresh grapefruit, with bacon and egg to follow. You wouldn't believe there was a war on, for all the food. I am making up for lost time. I hope the soldiers are getting some of it too.*
>
> *Through the window I can see first of all the sea, which is a bit rough, and then in the distance the next ship in the convoy. It is a comfort to see it, just in case we run into any problems. Though by the time you read this, any such problems will be over with.*
>
> *I have met a nice couple called the Richardsons. She is nice, anyway, and Mr Richardson is quite important. He writes for the newspapers. He tells us it is to be a quick passage. Eighteen days more, all being well.*
>
> *Could you send my best regards to Mrs Williamson and to the Tierneys? I didn't have time to say goodbye to them. I slept soundly and I didn't have any nightmares . . .*

She paused, wondering how her mother would manage; who she would find to listen to her, comfort her.

. . . I hope you have not had any either. I hope that Mrs
Gray is looking in each day like she promised . . .

She put down her pen and looked at the strangers eating breakfast nearby at the other tables: a middle-aged couple, two elderly gentlemen, a clergyman and a woman who was surely his sister, not his wife, a couple of men in smart suits. None of them needed her; when she got up, nobody would ask her where she was going; or how long she would be; or whether they could join her in her bed that night if sleep was hard. She could do as she chose. She was no longer the one who remained. She would have preferred not to be travelling during a war, but just now she would rather be here, in a convoy, hoping a U-boat didn't find them, than back at home with her mother. She smiled, thinking this. It was something she could never explain, not even to George. Especially not to George.

After breakfast, the siren rang for the lifeboat drill. Meg went to the day lounge, which was her muster station. She wore her new winter coat beneath the lifejacket. The lifejacket, with four big cubes of cork around the neck, made it difficult to move easily. But she had been told to put it on, as she would if there were a real emergency. The lounge was full. Women carried their handbags, like pantomime penguins in their cork jackets, and men smoked pipes or cigarettes. Mr Richardson made notes in a small notebook. A group of four still played bridge at one end. Somebody picked out a tune on the piano. Everybody had to attend the drill, unless they were ill. Meg's lifeboat was Number Six, port side. The Richardsons were to go to Number Eight.

'Coffee together afterwards,' Mrs Richardson said.

Meg went out onto the promenade deck with the other Number Six passengers. The officer in charge explained that if they had to evacuate the ship, each lifeboat would have a number of sailors and a number of passengers. Further down the deck was another group of passengers beneath another lifeboat, and beyond them she glimpsed some soldiers. Number Six lifeboat hung ten feet or more above them, level with the boat deck. She looked up at it while an officer went through the drill: how it would be lowered on its davits till it was level and they would get in. Then the designated lifeboat crew would lower it to the water, shimmy down the falls – those were the ropes – before unclipping them; how it contained food and water, first-aid equipment, eight oars to row with – best leave them to the sailors – and flares for getting rescued. How they were to follow instructions from the duty officer, which would probably be him. It was all very organised. Meg looked around at the other passengers. They were listening attentively; she supposed they felt their lives might depend on it.

There was something homely about the lifeboat, she thought, with its white overlapping planking, solid and fresh-painted. It was like a garden shed hung up there. But she couldn't imagine sitting in it; not out here in the middle of the ocean. It looked far too small to stay above the water.

∽

Each morning there was lifeboat drill and Meg grew accustomed to the idea of launching into the ocean in something so
small. The Captain had explained on the first night that it would
take five days' journey to sail beyond range of the U-boats.
When they reached that point, their destroyer escorts would
turn back and they would go on their merry way to South
Africa. As the first calm day gave way to the next, and that to
the next again, as those passengers who suffered seasickness
recovered and the privations and pressures of wartime
England receded, a holiday spirit began to spread among the
passengers. They were so nearly out of danger, Meg thought,
and it became harder each day to imagine something coming
upon them out of the blue and blowing it all apart. Even the
news from home seemed inflected by their mood, as though
the RAF had them, chugging their way across the Atlantic, to
thank for recent triumphs in the skies over London.

The days passed, the sea stayed calm and the lifeboats with
their shiny white hulls stayed suspended. Meg had settled in
to life on the ship with surprising ease. But though each day
might be a day closer to safety, it was also a day closer to her
marriage; and she knew, as well as she allowed herself to, that
she didn't love George.

On the third day Meg took coffee with Mrs Richardson, as
her habit now was, after the lifeboat drill. They sat outside,
just warm enough. Meg turned her face to the sun for its bit
of heat.

'I was thirteen when I saw the sea for the first time,' Meg
said. She made her voice bright because she was telling a story.

They sat in deck chairs and sipped coffee. Mrs Richardson had her hair caught up in a bandana and a silk wrap draped around her shoulders. She wore red slacks, and a grey sweater belonging to Mr Richardson. Meg thought she looked very sophisticated.

'The vicar's wife organised a day trip for the village children,' she said.

'You'd never seen the sea before?' Mrs Richardson said. 'I can't imagine.'

'Everybody else ran straight down to the water. I stood up on the promenade. Mrs Rogers – the vicar's wife – she had to persuade me. She said afterwards that I stood there with my mouth open.'

She draws a circle on the glass where it's misted. It's going to be a mouth with eyes but it drips down to the sill and becomes a spider. Through the window she sees her dad and there is Will hop-skipping, down to the end of the road over the white snow; they go around the corner.

She makes another spider on the window. It squeaks when she presses it with her finger tip. She watches the corner. A man goes past the window and then a woman. Jimmy Tullock and John Tullock go past. They run, because they are late for school, like always.

She drags a chair to the coat hooks and pulls down her coat. In the kitchen her mother cries. It's cold because the fire isn't lit this morning. Her mother has the matches and she is lighting and burning them so they are black from tip to tail. One, and then another, and another.

'You can save a sailor if you burn the whole match,' her mother says

in her normal voice, but there are still tears coming out of her eyes.

'I saw the Tullocks, so I'm going to school now,' Meg says.

She strokes her mother's lap; she can't see where the hurt is. She goes and fetches the plaid rug off the old chair where her father always sits. Bits and crumbs fall on the floor. It's heavy and it smells of tobacco.

'This will make you better,' she says.

She pulls and heaps it on her mother's lap.

'There now,' she says. 'Bye bye.'

Outside Meg walks beside her brother's footprints until she reaches the road. Now there are lots and she doesn't know which are his. The snow goes on and on, as far as she can see. It doesn't have any edges.

'I can't imagine,' Mrs Richardson said again. 'Your mother never took you? No seaside holidays?'

'No.' Meg sipped her coffee and looked out across the waves. It was odd, this talking to strangers. Back home she would never have done it. She would never have met Mrs Richardson back home, and once they were in Africa, they would probably never meet again.

'Can you swim?' she said.

'Like a fish,' Mrs Richardson said, 'but makes no difference either way, as long as you've got your life jacket on. So our sailor always insists. So I tell Mr Richardson. He doesn't want to carry his life jacket around.'

'I wish I could, even so,' Meg said.

Mrs Richardson stood up and excused herself. 'Must go and see what my husband is up to.'

Meg was getting cold, sitting so still. She wrapped her hands tight beneath her armpits. She had never had so much time and so little to do with it. She should be enjoying it, for all they were at sea and there was a war on.

In eleven days they would arrive. George would meet her and soon after they would marry. He had bought Meg's wedding ring already. It had cost £5 – he'd underlined the figure in his letter – and it was waiting for her in Africa. He was looking forward to putting it on her finger. He was looking forward to her being Mrs George Garrowby.

She should write a bit more to her mother. She picked up her handbag and lifejacket and nodded to the other deckchairs. She should go inside, but she didn't want to, and instead she set off towards the other end of the ship, ducking quickly under the rope cordon half way along.

She was nearly there when she saw the soldiers. Along walkways, up ladders, down steep metal stairs, her shoe heels clanging. It shouldn't have been such a shock.

They had their backs to her, hundreds of them. She could have counted, rows by columns, multiplied them. They were doing a drill, lifting guns up and down, while an officer shouted from the far end. She'd seen plenty of men in uniform in the last year. Each of the boys from the village got his farewell down the main street. But she'd known them; been at school with most of them. These were strangers.

She narrowed her eyes and stared. Two in the back row: they were the right build. She had to guess – she always had to guess – but she was sure he'd be about that height. Middling, her mother called it, like her. And one of them had the same kind of hair. It was darker, but his would be darker now, too. Her mother used to make a circle with her finger in his hair: 'Crown fit for a king,' she used to say.

There was another in front of them, a ginger-haired boy. He looked nothing like Will; was too young probably, yet . . . She narrowed her eyes still further, till the soldiers were no more than a series of grainy movements. What was it about him? If he were two foot smaller and if his gun were a stick and his uniform a pair of pyjamas, and if he didn't have ginger hair, then . . .

'You'd think the stick was his life.' She could hear her mother's voice. It was the same voice she'd use when Will got muddy, or tore his clothes.

'Boys will be boys,' Meg said to herself.

That was how the ginger-haired soldier held his gun, too, close-in to his head, caressing almost.

There was nothing about George that reminded her of Will. She'd never thought this before, but it was true.

The officer shouted and the soldiers wheeled. She felt the clap of their hands and the beat of their boots. She'd know him anywhere: by the curve of his brow, or how he walked, or by his eyes; she knew she would. Her mother's fingers in his hair and Will pulling away, impatient to be off, away on his adventure.

They were so handsome in their uniforms; alive and strong and on their way to fight. Each time something caught her eye – a turn of the head, the light on their hair – she'd look again, because it might be . . .

Then she'd look away.

Again a shout, again the soldiers wheeled round, shouldering, unshouldering; as he came to the head of the line, the ginger-haired soldier looked up at her, and she turned and went.

In her cabin she did as her mother would have told her and shut the blind over the porthole and lay down for twenty minutes. The air was warm, but she was shaking, so she pulled a blanket over, tucking it up beneath her chin, catching it under her feet.

The bed lamp made a small, safe circle and she was at the heart of it. She opened the bible and read about Jacob tricking his brother, then wrestling with the angel. There had been a picture of Jacob and the angel on the Sunday School wall. Alice said they were kissing.

Meg woke late in the afternoon. Her mouth was dry and she felt nauseous. She got up, ran a deep bath and lay submerged till her skin puckered in the warm salt water. She felt sad and though the water grew cold, it was a struggle to get out. Before going to dinner she wrote a few lines to her mother:

> *. . . I saw the soldiers parading today and thought of the lads in the village going off. James Pedley, and the Andrews boys especially. Please write to me with any news of them.*
>
> *It's funny but it doesn't feel dangerous on this ship. Perhaps because it's so luxurious, and because we have been lucky with*

the weather. But I have had enough of it and wish we could
be there sooner, for all the lovely food and time.

She went to dinner early to avoid the Richardsons, and sat
at a table between two elderly gentlemen. They told stories
about cricket and diamond mining and they let her be. She
was served with Lancashire hot pot and ice cream with tinned
peaches, but though she tried, she didn't manage to eat much.
Still she nodded and laughed when it was expected and the
meal passed off all right.

She saw the Richardsons across the room, and nodded and
smiled to Mrs Richardson. There was no reason she could put
her finger on, but she didn't want to speak with her, so she
excused herself to the old gentlemen and slipped away.

Two more days passed and Meg still kept her distance. The
soldiers parading had distressed her, and she needed time to
let her feelings settle. As much as possible, she sat outside.
Sometimes she liked to stand in the face of the wind and feel
the tears forced from her; or open her mouth and drink it in.
But mostly she would find secluded spots where she could be
on her own and just let the time go by. She slept thick, dream-
less sleeps, waking exhausted as if she had run for miles in her
head.

On the third day she sat down to lunch with the Richardsons.
They were already eating their soup. Mrs Richardson smiled
a greeting and Mr Richardson pulled out her chair, then shuffled it in from behind, as if he was locking her in to her place.

She'd decided not to tell them about seeing the soldiers,

but now, seated there, she wanted to please them; she wanted to give them something. She also wanted to drown out the sound Mr Richardson was making with his soup, and before she could check herself, the words were out.

'I came across the soldiers a few days ago,' Meg said. 'After our coffee. They were doing their drill.'

'Really?' said Mrs Richardson. 'You found them after we had coffee?'

'I carried on along that deck and eventually . . .'

'Should you have done that? Isn't that beyond where we're meant to go?'

'I just wanted to walk as far as I could,' Meg said. 'I felt a bit cooped up.'

'You're very daring,' Mrs Richardson said, smiling and shaking her head. 'Can't leave you alone for five minutes.'

Mr Richardson tapped his spoon against the bowl, pointed it at his wife.

'You're not to copy Margaret and go off wandering. One of us doing that sort of thing is quite enough.'

'Meg, not Margaret,' Meg said.

'Were they good at marching?' Mrs Richardson said.

'They looked very well-trained.'

Mr Richardson snorted slightly. 'How would either of you know?'

Meg shrugged and turned to Mrs Richardson. 'What will you do in South Africa?'

'She'll be inspecting the guard,' Mr Richardson said, 'won't you, darling?'

The steward brought Meg's soup and she was glad of an excuse to lower her head.

'John,' Mrs Richardson said. 'Meg was making conversation. She's just a girl.'

Mr Richardson pursed his lips. 'There's a reason why they keep the soldiers at the other end of the ship.'

Mrs Richardson put a hand over Meg's. 'Don't mind him. It's only his bark.'

The steward brought steak and kidney pudding and after he'd gone, Mrs Richardson continued. 'To answer your question, I'm going to be spring-cleaning when we get home. Have the house spick and span again. Two years away, it'll have gathered quite a lot of dust.'

'Be jolly glad to have you back where I know you're safe,' Mr Richardson said. 'Much rather you were polishing teaspoons than hiding in Anderson shelters.'

He turned to Meg and cocked his head slightly in what she took for a placatory gesture. 'I expect your fiancé will feel the same way, once this boat arrives.'

Meg nodded.

'I think you're jolly brave; I wouldn't do it on my own,' Mrs Richardson said.

Meg shrugged. 'George can't keep me safe.'

'You're just not used to it,' Mrs Richardson said. 'Growing up without your father. You're not used to having a man to look after you.'

∾

It's their morning game, before he does his shaving. But today she says 'Pa' to him and he doesn't look at her. He's smoothing his hair down with his fingers.

She pulls at his trouser leg.

'I'm your Princess Margaret,' she says, 'and you've rescued me from in the thorny thicket.'

He looks down then, but he doesn't smile.

'Meg,' he says.

'I'm Princess Margaret.'

He says 'Meg' again. He wipes his fingers and lifts her up and holds her close.

'You're hurting,' she says because he's squeezing her too tight, and he puts her down and picks up his razor.

Will is still asleep but she wakes him up.

'Play with me,' she says.

Then her pa comes in with foam on his cheeks and speaks to Will.

'Get dressed, quick as you can. We're visiting Ada. Nice and warm.'

'Can I get dressed nice and warm?' Meg says, but her pa's face goes angry and he bangs their door.

Will gets dressed.

'Play with me,' Meg says. But Will pulls on his brown sweater and goes downstairs.

'This ship,' Meg said. 'It's like a waiting room.'

Mrs Richardson patted her hand. 'You'll be busy soon enough, once the ring's on your finger.'

'That wasn't what I meant,' Meg said.

'Quite a fierce little thing, aren't you,' said Mr Richardson.

'Housekeeping is more than a full-time occupation,' Mrs Richardson said, ignoring her husband, 'especially when you're first married. I expect your mother's given you some good tips?'

'I know how to keep house.'

'A homebody then. That'll be useful in Africa,' said Mr Richardson.

'Finding out how your husband likes things; I had no idea how Mr Richardson liked his eggs boiled, or his shirt sleeves folded.'

'I know how,' Meg repeated.

'Only, what with your father not being there growing up . . .'

Meg turned to look Mrs Richardson straight in the face.

'It's not only husbands and fathers that need looking after. Excuse me, but I don't want to talk about marriage any more. Or housekeeping.'

She picked up her knife and fork. She could see the Richardsons exchange glances, and Mrs Richardson shrug. The pale suet was heavy in her mouth and hard to swallow.

'Another day and the convoy will be out of U-boat range. Then you ladies can relax. Plan your menus,' Mr Richardson said.

She closed her eyes. Shirts, and eggs, and knives and forks, and ice and cold, and sheets and blankets. Behind her, her mother cried at the kitchen table, and ahead of her was George.

'Meg?' said Mrs Richardson.

'Excuse me,' she said. Her feet were like lead beneath the

table and she couldn't breathe. She needed air. She shoved her chair out and stood. Mr Richardson had got up and a steward was approaching.

If she could just get away from everybody, she'd be all right again. Pushing past the steward she made for the lobby doors.

'Miss Bryan?' she heard, 'Miss Bryan? . . .'

She ran without looking, without caring, through doors, down stairways and along one passage after another, seeing nobody and paying no heed to signs, till the only sounds in her head were the deep roar of the ship and her own harsh breathing. At last she stopped, her head spinning, and leaned back against the bulkhead to get her breath. She thought she must be deep below the surface of the sea. The corridor was narrow and pipes ran along the ceiling; the lights cast a dim glow, pulsing slightly. It felt almost homely and it reminded her of somewhere; she laughed, her voice echoing back from the riveted walls. It was six days since she had left home, and eight since she had milked cows. How strange to think of that barn now, with its steamy half light and those heavy, warm animals. She knew her way round the barn with her eyes shut. And here she was, deep in this ship and she had no idea where she was, or what she was doing. Her laugh became a sob, her legs went to jelly and she slid down the wall.

She opened her eyes: black boots and khaki trousers. There was a hand on her shoulder; she could feel the fingers pressing.

She started and the hand lifted off.

'You shouldn't be down here, Miss.'

The voice was soft with an accent she didn't recognise.

'You all right?'

He sounded young.

'I got lost,' she said after a moment. She went to get up but her legs were still like jelly.

'I don't feel very steady.'

'Here,' the voice said, 'I'll give you a hand.'

She hadn't seen the man's face yet; and although she knew plenty of young men in the village, she never got this near to them. George was the only man she had been this near to. The thought of him just now made her shudder. If he could see her, he'd be shocked.

'We'll take it slow,' the soldier said.

He bent and took her hands.

'Easy,' he said. 'No rush.'

He was close as breathing and he smelt of damp wool and coal tar soap.

Her head swam and her fingers tingled, as though she had held them for an hour above her head. She stood up and leaned against the wall, staring at the floor, at his boots and her shoes, waiting for her sight to clear.

'Breathe, nice and deep, in through your nose and out through your mouth,' he said.

'I'm feeling steadier,' she said after a minute. 'I'll be fine in a . . .'

'Just wait here,' he said. 'I'll be back.'

Then as suddenly as he'd come, he went; she hadn't even seen his face. He might have been one of the soldiers she'd watched parading. Perhaps he'd watched her arrive on the tender. She kicked her heel at the wall. She was betrothed; she shouldn't be here, where a soldier could find her like this. Because of George she had left her mother; he had plans and when he told her, his eyes shone. He told her he would teach her and she would learn; he would help her smooth the rough edges and show her how to find her place. But she must do as he said, and he wouldn't like her being here like this.

Somebody else might find her, not a young soldier, but an officer; somebody who'd be angry, who'd rebuke her. Then the Richardsons might hear about it, and she'd be humiliated. She didn't know how to find her way back, but waiting felt unbearable, and she was about to leave when the soldier returned, and this time she saw him properly.

'I've checked and there's no one about right now. So shall I walk you home?' he said.

He was tall, taller than George, or Mr Richardson, taller than Will would be; and he had wide cheekbones and blue eyes. His hair was blond but the shadow on his jaw was dark and his eyebrows made two black lines across his brow. He wasn't like the boys at home. He looked foreign to her; he looked like a Viking, or how she imagined a Viking to look.

'Won't you get into trouble?' she said.

He grinned. 'Quick then, before they find I'm gone.'

Forgetting her embarrassment, Meg laughed. 'You remind me of my brother,' she said.

'How's that then?'

He knows how to get away with things.'

'He in uniform too?'

She shrugged, not a yes or a no.

'What about your fiancé?' he said, glancing at her engagement ring.

She nodded.

'Uniform makes us all look the same,' the soldier said. 'Anyway, the coast's clear. Let's go.'

'Do you know the way?'

But she followed him as if he did, and he walked ahead of her as if it were the most natural thing in the world.

It took them no time to get back to her part of the ship. More than once they passed sailors and she watched his shoulders gather authority so that he might have been on a mission for Churchill himself, the way he marched. Nobody stopped them; nobody asked what they were doing, though Meg felt herself blush to the roots each time. Then they reached the far end of her corridor.

'I know where I am now. My cabin's down here,' she said.

'I'll show you to your door.'

'But if a steward . . .'

'There's enough that's dangerous going on; at least I can show you to your door.'

There was a touch of grievance in his voice, so she let him. So much at stake for each if they were caught, it was better not to think about it, and they walked along the corridor, with the pictures of Naples and Nice hanging on the walls, and the war going on just out there, for all the world as if he were walking her home from the pictures.

'It's here,' she said.

She put her key in the lock and looked round.

'You've been . . .' she said, but he put a finger to his lips.

'What is it?' she whispered.

'Voices,' he whispered back.

She froze, listening, like a rabbit in the field when it hears the gun. Then turned the key and shoved the door with her shoulder.

'Quick,' she said, and she grabbed his sleeve. He stumbled against her and she fought to keep her feet, finding herself half-pinioned against the dressing table. The voices were clearer now and she knew them.

'The Richardsons. Shut the door,' she said. She passed him the key. 'Lock it.'

'Silent as the grave,' he said.

They stood stock-still in the dark, his hand on Meg's arm and her elbow banging against his ribs. She gripped the dressing table for balance. The tip of his boot dug at her ankle, so that she breathed rapidly and shallowly, so as not to exclaim or cry out.

The voices stopped outside her door.

'Meg!' Mrs Richardson called, then a pause. 'Meg!' she called again.

'Miss Bryan,' Mr Richardson said in an ordering tone of voice.

Meg held the dressing table tight, her palms slippy with sweat.

'If she's not here, then I shall speak to the captain.' Meg could hear every word; Mrs Richardson's voice was peremptory. 'He ought to know that a young woman has gone missing.'

'She'll be hiding out somewhere. She's only been gone half an hour.'

'But what if she isn't? She seemed very upset.'

'Silly little thing. There is a war on.'

'John!'

'Can't turn the ship, the bloody convoy, around for a single girl in the middle of the Atlantic.'

'John, don't.'

'She got herself worked up, God knows why. She'll be better once she's married,' he said.

Meg's mouth had dropped in surprise. It wasn't comfortable, hearing herself talked about like this. It wasn't comfortable, standing here in the dark with this stranger.

'Bang on the door, darling,' Mrs Richardson said. 'Just in case. She might be a heavy sleeper.'

The door thudded, a dull, underwater sound, then the door handle turned. Meg's heart was in her mouth. What if the soldier hadn't locked the door properly? But the door stayed firmly shut, and after a moment she heard Mr Richardson's voice again.

'Come on. I want a cup of coffee, before the steward's buggered off.'

It went quiet after that, but she couldn't tell if they'd gone. What if they were waiting in the corridor? She listened out as hard as she could beyond the sound of her own breathing but all she could hear was the ship's noisy silence gathered around them – its deep turbine rumble, the break of sea against the hull. With her body jarred against the soldier's – elbow and shoe and hip and chin — she waited until she thought she couldn't bear it any longer, that she would snap with the tension. Then the soldier spoke.

'Phew,' he said.

That was all; that was it. The Richardsons had gone, and like fugitives who've evaded capture, a delirium rose in them that was irresistible and absolute. Their laughter exploded. It took them like a seventh wave, crashing through so that they collapsed to the floor, his hand finding her face, her arm across his chest. Limbs flailing and weak, they laughed in the darkness till they wept. They laughed in the darkness till Meg was faint and light, as if she'd just come out of a fever. She couldn't move, or speak; she couldn't think. She was suspended above her life: above the ship and the war, above George and her marriage, and the Richardsons and her mother. Then silently, ineluctably, hand to hand, mouth to mouth, moving by touch and gauge, they kissed, and kissed again. She felt his cheek, wet with tears, soft with fine stubble, and his mouth, and his chin and ears. His hands were on her face, and her shoulders; they were on her breasts.

There on the hard linoleum floor, they tumbled in the dark, urgent and exhilarated, tugging at buttons, pulling at rough khaki and smooth stockings. Meg's heart was a drum and her blood rushed. She reached and pulled him down on to her, butting her head into his shoulder, wanting his weight, wanting the press of his hips. Then she felt with her fingers till she found him, so hard and full that she gasped, because she didn't know men did this; and she drew him in to her, crying

out because it hurt, even while she wanted it. Right now she
wanted it more than anything else in the world. She held him
and he moved inside her; she held him and cried out, and they
became their own wave.

Afterwards, everything was very still. Slowly, reluctantly,
she returned to herself, back into her cabin, and her body,
back to what had just happened.

'Oh God,' she said quietly.

Her hand lay flat on the soldier's chest and his heart beat
against her fingers. After a time he lifted and kissed them,
then he let go and she heard his boots creak.

'I'll put on the light,' he said.

'No!' she cried, her voice panicked. 'Don't! Don't go,' and
the words shocked her because they came from deep down,
out of something much older than this sharp passion.

'I have to,' he said gently, and a moment later the cabin
swam in dim light.

She stood and in the mirror she saw herself, and him behind
her. His face was grave, and so was hers; next to the mirror
was George in his frame, and he seemed to Meg like someone
she had never seen before.

'I don't know your name,' she said.

'Are you all right?' he said.

'You have to go,' she said, and she wanted it to be a question, but it was impossible.

'Sergeant Jim Cooper,' he said.

She turned around to face him.

'I'll be married a week from now.'

He nodded.

'And I'll be fighting, like as not.'

'I don't want you to go, Jim Cooper. We weren't found, and then this happened.'

She stepped close and pulled his tunic straight and fastened the buttons. Picking his belt off the floor, she pulled it around his waist. He didn't take his eyes from her face.

'Just your hair now,' she said and she watched as he bent to the mirror and with a lick to his fingers, smoothed it into place. Then he touched her cheek softly.

'What should we say?'

She didn't reply; only kissed him on the lips, unlocked the door and looked quickly each way to make sure it was clear. Then he was gone.

Afterwards Meg slept, for five minutes, or an hour, or three hours, she didn't know, and when she woke, she was famished. It was imperative, like a child's hunger. She must have food, and she remembered her mother's cake, baked for Meg's wedding. They'd eaten a piece each before Meg left, then her mother had divided the rest between them. She was to keep her chunk for her wedding day, but now she opened her trunk, unwrapped it and ate nearly all of it. It quelled the hunger though she still felt hollow. Hollow and tender. She touched herself between the legs and her fingers came away a little bloody. Alice said this always happened to you the first time. It was how your husband knew you'd kept yourself for him. But the man who had made her bloody was not the man she was to marry. The man who had made her bloody she would probably never see again. She looked at George's photo and placed it face down on the dressing table.

She needed to tidy up, collect herself and go and show herself, before the Richardsons came back with a deputation. The bathroom was cold and in the mirror Meg saw a pale-faced girl who blushed when she caught her eye. She ran a basin of water and gently she wiped herself with a flannel, wincing a little with the salt. The blood coloured the basin water pink.

She would have changed her clothes, but it might have invited a comment from Mrs Richardson. So she only changed her underwear. She thought: I shouldn't be doing this; I should be ashamed. George's photo looked uncomfortable, set down like that, like a creature fallen over that couldn't get to its legs, so she placed it upright again. Then she brushed her hair, powdered her face, did her lipstick, and dabbed a little perfume on her wrists in case she smelt of something. Tidying up the cabin, she set George's photo glass down again. She didn't feel ashamed; not one bit. But she didn't need to rub his face in it.

The lounge was nearly empty, only two people at the far side. Meg sat down in the opposite corner and took out the letter to her mother:

We are six days out and any minute now we will be safe from U-boats. Mr Richardson says this is a fact. The Richardsons have been very kind and I take many of my meals with them. The weather is quite warm now. I have sat out on deck more. At the back of the ship there are

*deckchairs, all put in lines by a steward for the morning
and higgledy-piggledy by lunch. I am getting nervous about
meeting George and being married so quickly and wish you
could be with me, and Alice as my maid-of-honour. Also I
wish Pa and Will were there. But I am sure I will be fine
when it comes to it, only a little sad to be on my own.*

She wrote the names 'Pa' and 'Will' slowly, like a child who
hasn't been long at its letters. Her ma wouldn't like reading
them, and Meg would never have said such a thing if she were
at home. She would never have dared. Pa and Will; Pa and
Will: the names they never spoke; the names she had whispered to herself all those years.

*The Yardleys is very nice and I am being careful, to make it
last . . .*

She sniffed her wrist. What was he doing now, Sergeant Jim
Cooper? Was he thinking about her? She stared at the sea,
the steepling waves; but she saw none of it and was lost in
her thoughts when the Richardsons found her and, taking an
armchair on each side, hemmed her in.

'Meg, dear. We've been so worried, ever since lunch and . . .'

'I'm fine,' Meg said. 'Look. Arms and legs.'

'Don't know what you have been playing at, but I saw
people dead in the Blitz,' Mr Richardson said. 'They didn't go
to the shelter, didn't play by the rules, so no one knew, next
thing was . . .' and he pulled a finger across his throat.

'John, please.'

'I've carried my life jacket everywhere,' Meg said.

'John's being melodramatic,' Mrs Richardson said. 'But we came to find you. We knocked on your door.'

'That's very kind of you.' Meg realised she'd been stupid not to work out her story earlier.

'I was going to speak to the Captain,' Mrs Richardson went on, 'but Mr Richardson said there was no point in worrying everybody before we were sure you were missing.'

Meg looked down, studying the table's polished surface. She felt a blush rise on her neck as she remembered Mr Richardson's actual words. 'I'm sorry you were so worried.'

'Only you left the table in something of a . . .' Mr Richardson said.

'Would you mind,' Meg said, breaking in, 'if I spoke to Mrs Richardson privately?'

Meg caught a swift look of gratification on Mrs Richardson's face. Her husband nodded shortly and walked over to the window. Meg leaned forward.

'Margery?' she said in a low voice. 'Can I ask your advice?'

'Of course.'

'It's ladies' trouble.'

'That's what happened over lunch?'

Meg nodded. 'It was very sudden, and I'm not due for a week.'

'Are you still?' Mrs Richardson said.

Meg shook her head.

Mrs Richardson leaned over and patted Meg's hand. 'I expect

it's anxiety; about the marriage. It can have a strange effect.'

Meg nodded, trying to adopt a suitable expression.

'We won't say any more about it.' Mrs Richardson gave Meg's hand a second pat.

'You're very kind,' Meg said.

With a wave to her husband, Mrs Richardson sat back in her chair.

'Wind's getting up,' Mr Richardson said, taking his seat again. 'I'd put it at 30 knots.'

'There's to be no more said,' said Mrs Richardson.

'Margaret's decreed, has she?' Mr Richardson raised his eyebrows. 'I only hope you weren't in your cabin after all, because we made the most frightful din.'

And he smiled a dangerous smile. But Meg had something to guard and she had discovered that she could be steely too; so she only smiled in return.

She's got her nose against the window but all there is, is black.

'Dark as the dead,' she says, like Aunt Ada.

The window is so cold, it makes her sneeze. Somebody knocks on the back door. Meg listens for her ma pushing her chair back and going to open it. They knock again, but her ma makes no noise. She doesn't move her chair back to stand and she doesn't open the door.

'There's someone knocking,' Meg says.

She knows it isn't Will, or her pa, because they wouldn't knock. But it might be Mrs Gray or Mrs Gilmer and maybe they might have seen Will or maybe they might have a bun or a biscuit, because sometimes they did have.

'I'm hungry,' Meg says.

She slides off the chair and runs into the kitchen.

'I'm hungry,' she says again.

Her ma still sits and she doesn't answer. There is nothing on the table except her ma's hands. Meg pulls at the door curtain and climbs around it and bangs back on the door with her fist.

'I'm here,' she calls out. 'I'm here.'

But they must have gone, because nobody answers.

'They won't be back,' her ma says.

Meg turns but her ma's face still doesn't do anything. It doesn't smile or frown, and it doesn't look at Meg.

'It's tea time,' Meg says, 'and it's dark outside; that's when my pa comes home from making his tables and chairs. And he's got Will too. You know he has.'

She gets out cutlery and puts it on the kitchen table, knives and forks in their places and a spoon extra for her. Will teases her because she gets them the wrong way about, but she won't mind him teasing her today when he is back from the adventure. Then cups and saucers and last of all the salt cellar. Where her ma's arms are, she puts the fork and knife each side. The table is ready. She waits a moment in case they come back home just then, before going upstairs.

The bedroom is very cold, and so is the bed. She pulls Will's pyjamas from under the pillow and puts them on the counterpane, a pile of arms and legs. There's a noise downstairs and she stops; but there aren't any voices, she doesn't hear Will's shout. They might be back any time because it's dark now, so the adventure must be over. She hopes it will be soon because she is very hungry. She makes Will's

pyjamas into a boy shape, ready and waiting, and pulling the counter-
pane over her, curls up beside them and closes her eyes.

The rest of that day, and the next, and the one after that, as
the sea remained calm and the weather grew warmer, as the
convoy steamed closer to Africa, and George, and for all those
soldiers buried deep in the bows, closer to the war, Meg waited
to meet Jim Cooper again. She was sure she would; it was a
conviction, lodged deep in her gut and she stayed prepared.
How carefully she dressed, in the blouse with the decorated
mother-of-pearl buttons; in stockings that she rinsed every
night; in the pretty knickers Alice had given her with a giggle
for her wedding day. She rinsed those, too, each night, and
pulled them on, still damp in the seams, in the morning.

'Smells like a tart's boudoir,' Mr Richardson said when she
came to breakfast the day after.

'John!' Mrs Richardson said. 'It's only Yardleys.'

But Meg didn't care. Because eating, chatting to other passengers, even sleeping, she was ready. Several times a day
she ran a basin of salt water, and gently she washed. She'd
never been so tender with herself before. She dressed from
her meagre wardrobe with Jim Cooper in her mind, as if he
would find her again and notice the pattern on her pearl buttons or that she had her hair in braids.

She imagined him everywhere. Imagined him appearing,
as if from nowhere: there in the dining room as she buttered
her toast; his head around the bathroom door smiling at her
naked in the bath; or bent over her while she slept, waking her

with a kiss. When she was little, she'd thought God was like a Mr Punch who could see you whatever you were doing and who might pop up anywhere, just when you weren't ready. Now Jim Cooper had become her God and she dreamed and dreamed of him catching her unawares.

But it was Mr Richardson she had to look out for. He was like a wolf and he knew she was hiding something. If she wasn't careful, he'd have her by the scruff and shake her till she dropped it. So she cultivated other acquaintances, sitting beside Reverend Lindsell while he taught her gin rummy, and listening to Miss Lindsell's stories of adventures in the Holy Lands, travelling with her brother.

'You're so lucky to be engaged,' Miss Lindsell said. She knitted, as she spoke, with great application.

'Mrs Gilmer used to say that knitting calmed the soul,' Meg said.

Miss Lindsell nodded. 'Very wise, and true for those of us who need to calm our souls. Old maids like me. But you'll be wed in a week. There's time enough for you to knit later.'

Meg looked at her lap. George would be so at ease in here, with the cigars and the taking of tea. She should school herself to it because very soon she would marry him, and she'd be willing to bet that she'd learn to knit sooner than Miss Lindsell thought. She'd bear his children and keep his house, and her life would be ordered and safe. No one would rush from the table in horror, or leave the house with no breakfast, or get lost.

But her new, fledgling self, the one that had wrestled with

Jim Cooper on the cabin floor, didn't care a fig about knitting, or safety. That new Meg wanted to stand in the middle of the lounge and laugh out loud.

On the eighth day Meg came to lunch to find a small crowd gathered around the Richardsons' table and Mr Richardson holding forth.

'It'll be given out later today; we're out of U-boat range,' Mr Richardson was saying, clipped and sure.

'How do you know?' Miss Lindsell said.

'Right place at the right time,' Mr Richardson said. 'I heard it from the horse's mouth.'

There was a flurry of clapping and he went on. 'We are beyond reach. Beyond their fuelling range. If you don't believe me, look out of the window. Our escort has turned back and we are now officially on a pleasure cruise.'

People looked out of the window and there was laughter and more clapping. Meg watched Mrs Richardson lean across and kiss her husband. The stewards brought in trays of champagne.

'Listening at other people's doors,' Meg muttered.

'We don't have to carry our lifejackets with us any longer,' Miss Lindsell said, handing Meg a glass. 'Champagne, courtesy of the Richardsons.'

'You wouldn't know there was a war, on this ship, except for all those soldiers up in the front,' Meg said.

'Your fiancé will be anxious, waiting for you. A shame you can't let him know you're safe,' said Miss Lindsell.

'Yes,' Meg said. 'It's a shame.'

She saw George ahead of her, pacing to and fro in the desert and checking on his watch – he was always checking on his watch – and a man on a horse galloping towards him with a note in his hand.

'If we are still in Cape Town, might I come to the wedding?'

'Yes,' Meg said. 'Of course.'

There was a party atmosphere on the ship that evening. A toast was made to the captain and officers and someone sang a ditty about devils and deep blue seas. Meg sat at the Richardsons' table once again. She had little appetite for the jollity, but she smiled and laughed nevertheless. Mr Richardson was the life and soul. He behaved as though he were somehow responsible for the ship's newfound safety. Meg caught him watching her now and then, but she had put on her plainest dress and forsworn the Yardleys. He had nothing to fault her with.

'You seem better,' Mrs Richardson said. She nodded towards her husband. 'He does mean well. He's just protective.'

Meg nodded too, then frowned. 'I don't need his protection,' she said, but she caught Mrs Richardson's expression and checked herself from saying more.

Later Meg walked alone outside. The moon was full and when the clouds parted, the ship was bathed in silver. The air had a foreign warmth and she took off her cardigan to feel the wind on her arms. She leaned against the rail and looked out to the horizon. The ship seemed so still in the sea, as though it too was suspended between one life and another. She wanted someone else to stand here with her; someone else to drink the air and wonder. She shut her eyes and though she knew he wouldn't be there, she couldn't stop a tiny hope.

'Jim Cooper,' she said to herself and again, louder: 'Jim Cooper.'

But soon she would be safe and married, and he would be gone.

10.30 pm.

Dear Ma,

There's been a party tonight because we're safe at last. Mr R tells us it's definite because we're beyond the 600-mile point. He overheard the captain say so. He says the U-boats can't get this far, because they haven't got enough fuel.

So I'm going to wear only my pyjamas in bed tonight. Phew, because it was getting rather hot with everything else on top.

In 8 days' time we'll be there. Then this letter can start its journey back to you. It's the longest one I've ever written and by the time you get it, I'll have been a married woman for at least a month. I can't imagine it.

She put the letter and pencil down beside the bunk, tucked her covers close around her and closed her eyes. The cabin was warm and a little airless and Meg felt secure. Although she hadn't felt sleepy, she was asleep in minutes.

She was dreaming, watching Errol Flynn kiss Olivia de Havilland, with George beside her upstairs in the Embassy. He had a bag of penny toffees and his hand was on her knee. The kiss went on and on until a 'boom' noise made the two lovers stop; then they got on to a motor bus, but couldn't find the fare and the conductor asked them to get off. But the strangest part of the dream, the part Meg never mentioned later, was that while George sat on one side of her, Jim sat on the other. She watched the two lovers kiss and Jim leaned towards her and whispered: 'Come with me,' and she turned, but it wasn't Jim any more. It was Will. Will smiling into the sun that shone from somewhere and beckoning to her.

Meg woke. Something had happened. She listened. Perhaps it was in her dream and she began to drift to sleep again. But then she heard it. Not a noise, but the absence of one. The ship's bass note – the deep 'dub, dub' throb – was gone. The engine had stopped. She opened her eyes. A flickering blue light came under the door and set the room in shadows and the air was acrid with a smell she didn't recognise. Somewhere close a bell was ringing, a shrill, insistent 'thrang' noise that went on and on.

In a single movement she was out of the bunk, wholly alert, clear-eyed. Something had happened, but she didn't know what or when. She needed to dress quickly and get out of there. She tried the lights but they weren't working. Moving round the shadows in the dark, she stumbled because the floor had tilted. Fumbling with the dresser drawers, she found a blouse and cardigan and pulled them on over her pyjamas, then her coat and finally the life jacket. The acrid smell grew stronger by the minute and she was sure the floor had tilted further. Reaching under her pillow she felt for the snapshot of her mother. Then she opened the cabin door.

The corridor was empty and Meg would have run except that the air was so smoky, she could barely see an arm's length ahead. She needed to find other people and for once she would have been happy to see even Mr Richardson. More by touch than by sight, she reached the stairs and climbed. Her mind was clear. She would not be left behind this time; she would not be left. At the top of the stairs the air was clearer. A sailor stood there and pointed her on towards the lounge.

'We'll be all set in a jiffy,' he said.

'But we've been hit?' Meg said, confused by his tone.

He nodded.

'Torpedoed. Number three hold, back in the stern. It's a big gash.'

'We're sinking?' Meg said.

'Captain's given the order to abandon ship. We're readying the lifeboats. Best if you joined the others,' the sailor said, pointing again.

As she crossed the lobby she thought of Jim Cooper and she kissed the air for him before putting her hand to the lounge door.

Meg stopped amazed in the open doorway. It was packed and she guessed she was the last to arrive, again. Candles stood slanted on every table, wax guttering down towards the sea; and the emergency lights sent out their blue glow, bathing the floor. People sat with bags and cases beside them and most wore their life jackets. But nobody seemed to be panicking. In fact the room had an air of last-chance hilarity, as if people were determined to carry on whatever. Someone even played the piano and a woman even sang:

And you think you're in the swim,
But the lights go dim,
And you're out on the tiles,
But it's raining in the aisles.
Oh my Honey Bee,
Oh my Fish in the Sea,
Hold tight and soon you'll be through...

At one table people were playing blackjack, reaching around their life jackets to fish out their stakes. There was a group drinking at the bar and Mr Richardson was playing the barman, pouring out measures of gin and whisky, handing out the change. She saw him check his watch, and check it again thirty seconds later, as though the ship were sinking to a timetable.

She looked around. In one corner Reverend Boondock was leading a prayer. Mrs Richardson must be here too, but she couldn't see her and for a moment she panicked. Surely he couldn't have left his wife in the cabin? But then she saw her, sitting at the end of a sofa at the far side with a pair of older ladies. Meg walked towards them. One of the ladies appeared to have put on all her jewellery, a thick string of pearls riding over the top of her life jacket and her arms jangling with gold. The other held her handbag in both hands, and Meg noticed that every so often she would stroke it, as if it were a pet in need of reassurance.

'The smell,' the pearl woman said. 'I know the smell.'

'They'll have radioed it by now,' the other said. 'We should be picked up very quickly.'

They, at least, weren't pretending.

Meg knelt down beside Mrs Richardson. She didn't have her life jacket. Meg saw she was shaking, clutching and reclutching her hands in her lap. Meg touched her.

'It'll be all right,' she said quietly. 'But your life jacket?'

'I'm a good swimmer,' Mrs Richardson said.

'Smells like the air raids,' the pearl woman said. 'Cordite. Sticks in your throat.'

'They'll rescue us,' Meg said.

'It's horrible,' the pearl woman said.

'I need a drink.' Mrs Richardson grabbed at Meg's hand. 'Get me a drink.'

Meg had to jostle a bit to get to the front of the bar. She'd never done this before; girls didn't, and if George could have seen her he'd have been cross. But it was an emergency and she put her hands on the counter and leaned in.

'Gin and tonic for your wife,' she said loudly.

She waited for Mr Richardson to turn towards her, to meet her eye.

'Damned thing, this,' he said to his listeners with an expansive gesture. 'Going to mess up my article deadlines.'

'Excuse me,' Meg said.

'Though I've got a fairly watertight excuse,' and he paused for a laugh at his joke. 'Sorry it's late. Got torpedoed.'

Sharp laughter bellied out around Meg.

'Your wife needs a drink,' she said, more loudly.

He acknowledged her then with a slight tip of the head and reached for the gin.

'Ice and lemon?'

'She's very frightened,' Meg said.

'Actually we're low on the ice.'

'Despite what you told us last night, the ship is sinking, and your wife needs you,' Meg said.

'Tell her I'll be over shortly.'

'She needs you now, and she needs her life jacket.' Meg turned away in such a fury that it took all her self-command not to hurl the drink in his face.

The ship had listed further in the last few minutes and now at last people had given up the performance of normality. They were picking up their bags; the blackjack game was abandoned and all at once even the bar was deserted.

Meg handed Mrs Richardson the glass.

'He'll be over in a moment,' she said.

She drank it down like water.

'Dutch courage,' she said. But she'd taken Meg's hand again and was gripping it even tighter.

Several of the ship's officers had come in and one looked to be issuing orders.

'Look,' Meg said. 'They'll have us in the lifeboats any time now.'

As if he had heard her, the officer addressed the passengers then.

'Please make your way to the deck, and go straight to your allocated lifeboat. We'll be lowering them immediately.'

Mr Richardson strode towards them and Meg prised her hand free.

'I must go,' she said. And as she turned away: 'I'll see you in Cape Town.'

Meg felt calm, stepping out onto the deck. She had on her life jacket and she was well drilled in what to do. Most importantly, she was on her own. And she knew how to be on her own. Nobody was holding her hand. In her pocket was her mother's photo, and she could see her now, standing at the kitchen window. That was how Meg always thought of her: looking away, looking out of that window.

The ship was lit in black and white by the moon and though the engines had died, it was still moving forward. Up here the smoke was thicker, gusting across the deck so that one minute you could see around you and the next you were lost. Groans rose from the ship's heart as if it were a great beast dreadfully wounded: echoing wrenching sounds. Sailors with torches moved around calmly, shouting instructions, and clumps of people waited patiently, their fear only visible in the way they gripped their bags, or drummed their fingers, or looked about, as if there might be some other place to go to, some way out of this.

Several lifeboats were already lowered to deck level, and small crowds were clustered at the rail. But with the ship at an angle, the boats were swinging out over the sea and nobody could board them. Meg watched the sailors lean out over the black ocean with boat hooks, hooking them round the falls to try and pull the lifeboats in. Miss Lindsell was there, handbag on one arm. She waved to Meg, quite as though they had passed on the street. She had her arm around someone's shoulder, and while Meg watched she clipped open her handbag and took out smelling salts.

Meg's lifeboat station, Number Six, was further down the promenade deck towards the stern and she stumbled on in that direction, clinging to the stanchions and rails as best she could to stop herself running headlong with the slope. She pictured the lifeboat – its solid planking, the tin cans of food, the bandages and blankets. It was just ahead of her, ready and waiting. The steam grew denser and the noise was thick in her ears, pushing out her thoughts; her feet slipped on the slick deck and she reached out into the air for something to hold.

'Watch out!'

As if from a long way off, the voice broke in. She grabbed at a length of flailing rope and froze. Invisible till now, with all the smoke and steam, just a few feet from her was a huge crater, a rupture reaching right across the deck. Thirty feet wide and as many down, it looked as if some savage giant had reached into the bowels and ripped the ship open. Metal was torn and crumpled like tissue paper, charred and broken. Electrical jags ran along the edges and somewhere deep down a fire was raging, sending up a pink glow and the smell that Meg recognised now as melting metal. She stared at the metal carnage and her stomach turned. This was in the soldiers' quarters.

She saw Jim bending towards her and taking her hands; she saw him in her cabin, his tunic tumbled, his eyes bright.

'Please God,' she murmured.

Her lifeboat, her safe journey, was blown apart, its solid white boards, its food and drink burnt up somewhere in that ghastly hole. She heard voices – screams and cries – from within the crater. They were distant and unearthly and she put her hands over her ears.

'Miss!' The sailor was shouting at her. 'Miss!'

'My lifeboat,' she said.

'Go back. Get in another one.'

'There are soldiers down there.'

'They're getting everyone out. You must get in a lifeboat.'

And he took her by the shoulders and pushed her away. 'Go!'

She looked out for Miss Lindsell, and for Mrs Richardson, but she didn't see them. The lifeboats were nearly all full. Passengers sat looking just as if they were on a bus trip to the seaside, rather than a lifeboat in the middle of the Atlantic, while the sailors worked the falls, lowering the boats to the sea. It was precarious. The ship was sinking now at such a pitch that they struggled to keep the lifeboats on an even keel. Once the boats were in the water, the sailors shimmied down rope ladders and unclipped the falls. Then they moved slowly away from the ship, drifting into the darkness.

It was as if Meg forgot herself, watching. Her urgency left her and she felt detached and calm. She should go and claim her place, take her seat like the others and clasp her baggage, like ballast, on her lap. But she had no baggage; there was nothing to anchor her. She didn't feel any despair; just the utter absence of any hope. And perhaps, if a sailor hadn't noticed her, she might have stayed on the ship and journeyed down with all the young soldiers she'd heard crying out.

'You hurt?' The sailor was yelling to make himself heard.

She shook her head.

'Number Three,' he said. 'Over there.'

So she took her seat in the bow and sat tight. There were soldiers on the deck, filling up the spare places. She could only see the faces nearest to her, but none of them was Jim. Just ahead Miss Lindsell was counseling courage to someone; it was reassuring to hear a voice she knew, and a female one. Meg watched a sailor lift her up and into the lifeboat, quite as if she were a child in the playground, and Miss Lindsell turn back to him and thank him gravely.

Several of the soldiers seemed to be injured and one sitting close to her smelled of engine oil. He was soaked to the skin and shaking. The boat was full. Sailors were busy with the falls, then Meg felt it move. It went down in short, jerky movements and with each one the wounded soldier made a quick groaning sound, as if somebody was squeezing the air from him. Meg gripped the seat. She didn't want to watch, but when she closed her eyes it was like being in a dream where up and down, and inside and outside, were all confused. So she opened them again and stared at her lap.

The lifeboat hung from the dying ship; above them, the sailors shouted into the wind: 'Hold in aft! Hold it in!'

'Easy, steady her off.'

The water was close – she could smell it. They'd be floating on the ocean in a minute.

'Steady, damn you!'

The sailor's voice was desperate and Meg looked up. His face, lit by the strange emergency blue, was a mask of terror. Then she screamed as the bow end of the lifeboat dropped down towards the sea. Flung forward, she smashed hard against the bench in front. She was stunned, the breath blown from her, and when she came to, she found her hand trapped painfully between the bench and her life jacket. She tried to shift, to ease the pressure, but the wounded soldier was thrown against her and she was pinioned. The smell of the oil turned her stomach, but she couldn't move. She saw people in the sea and they were those same people who had sat so neatly on their benches moments before. No wounded soldier to pinion them, they'd been flipped from the boat like so many matches. She heard their cries, their shouts for help. One of the voices was Miss Lindsell's.

The sailors pulled at the ropes and somehow the lifeboat was levelled off again and lowered finally to the water. The sailors dropped down the rope ladders, unhitched the falls and the lifeboat floated free. Meg felt the wounded soldier shift; then his weight was off her and he half-crouched, half-lay against the side of the boat. He was murmuring, but not to her and when she spoke to him, he didn't hear her. Pulling herself up, she gripped the edge of the lifeboat and called out: 'Miss Lindsell!'

The sea had looked so calm that evening. But the waves rose like small gullies now and the lifeboat crashed over and down, over and down. Some of the people in the water had managed to swim back and they were being hauled in: five, six, seven of them. But none was Miss Lindsell.

'Miss Lindsell!' Meg shouted again, but Miss Lindsell and her handbag and her courtesy had gone.

Somebody took charge.

'Hands to the rowing gear,' he shouted. 'We need to get clear or she'll take us all down with her.'

Soldiers scrambled to the pump handles and Meg sat down again. Slowly the boat moved away.

She doesn't have her coat on but her ma doesn't see. It's dark outside except that the snow makes things show up suddenly. Trees and walls and other things. Meg runs to catch up. She does it in little steps like Will has showed her because it's slippy on the snow, but she falls down once and gets her hands wet.

'Wait. I'm coming too.'

Left and right, left and right they look. They go up the lane and over the road towards the school. They go all the way to the bridge. They go up to the church gate and round the churchyard walls.

'Dark as sin,' her ma says.

'Will!' Meg calls. 'Will!' and the snow swallows up the sounds. Meg calls out 'Pa!' too. Her ma doesn't call.

Nobody answers; there's only an animal with yellow eyes that runs away in the ditch. Meg's feet hurt in her boots and her toes are sticking together.

'Can we go home?' she says. 'I'm cold,' and she takes her ma's hand. 'See?' But she can't make her ma's fingers bend around hers.

'You're not holding,' she says and her ma looks down at her all of a
sudden, and then they go back.

Meg looked at the ship and, as if on cue, it lit up like Christmas,
every light on deck blazing down on the water. It had tipped
so far now, it looked like a shining iceberg, throwing a pool
of light across the sea. It was terrible and beautiful. And there
were all the other lifeboats, each crammed with heads. Surely
Jim is in one of them, she thought, and though she had no faith
in the prayer, she prayed to God to keep him safe.

Only a single boat remained close to the ship. Meg could
almost see the faces at the nearer end. There were people
on the oars and yet it wasn't moving. She saw one man push
another off an oar and take over; she saw another stop and
throw up his arms and cover his head. The ship would sink
very soon now and if nothing happened, then all those people
would be sucked down with it.

She watched the figures abandon the oars and several
people jump over the side and begin swimming. Two figures
started fighting. Then she heard a voice she knew, small inside
the wind, but still she could hear that it was angry, and she saw
that the Richardsons were in the middle of that boat.

Mrs Richardson was standing still, no lifejacket, her arms by
her sides, and Mr Richardson was yelling. He grabbed at her and
tried to pull her to the edge, but she fought him and screamed.

'Jump, Margery,' Meg whispered. 'You can swim.'

But Mrs Richardson went on standing and screaming, and
Mr Richardson went on shouting.

'Pull her into the sea,' Meg yelled. 'Just pull her.'

The ship had seemed to pause in its sinking, as if it were gathering itself up for the final push, and now a sound came from it that was like a vast sigh.

It was a terrible sight. They jumped and scrambled and tumbled into the sea, and some came up and swam and some never did; and some got away and most didn't.

Finally Mr Richardson let go of his wife and kissed her on the forehead. He climbed up on a bench, coattails flapping, and dived. Mrs Richardson still stood, looking towards the ship, one hand on a useless oar for balance.

Mrs Richardson's lifeboat was nearly touching it when at last the ship lifted its bright bow to the dark sky, and as if it were the easiest thing in the world, the ship, and the boat, and the single woman standing, slid beneath the sea.

The ship lights shone beneath the water for a while, then everything went black. And monstrous waves rolled out from where the ship had been, tossing the lifeboat so hard, Meg feared it would capsize. Voices still cried out for help. She couldn't tell where they were. Some got to Meg's lifeboat and were pulled in, but it wasn't long before the cries stopped. Debris bumped the boat for a while – deckchairs and timber. Once Meg saw a body bang against the side. Then the sea was empty again. She listened, but there was nothing to see, and nothing to hear except the waves and the wind.

The boat drifted, and Meg drifted too, her back to the black ocean, half-sleeping, half-waking. Once she thought she heard

Jack's voice. She was cold, her face, her feet, her hands: all numb; she didn't think, and she didn't dream. In one pocket her fingers made a cold fist around her mother's photograph. Beside her, the wounded soldier groaned in his delirium. Once or twice someone fed him brandy; once someone passed her a beaker with water and she drank it down and asked for more, but no more came.

The dawn woke her properly, first a grey ribbon on the edge of the horizon, then the lifeboat floating in gold. They were alone on the sea, no other boats, nothing that showed any sign of the ship. She was stiff and cramped and she longed to stretch out her legs, and swing her arms. But the wounded soldier leaned against her and he had gone quiet, his eyes closed, his face bone-white and peaceful. Carefully she bent and put her face close to his and listened. He was still breathing, though his breath smelled rank. She couldn't move without disturbing him, so she stayed as she was, only turning her head to look around.

She could see the lifeboat properly for the first time, now it was light. A sailor sat up as look-out, but most people seemed to be still sleeping, or dozing, or too exhausted to move, perhaps. She wondered who had passed her the beaker during the night because she had a raging thirst now, and she was hungry. It was difficult to see exactly how many people there were, because they were jammed in every which way, and some lay on the bottom of the boat. But she had a go at counting the heads and got to over forty. As far as she could see it was mostly soldiers, and a few sailors. There were no other civilians; there were no other women. As she watched, a figure in an overcoat, up in the bows, sat up off the floor, wrapped his arms around his body and looked across the sea.

'Mr Richardson!' Meg exclaimed.

He turned slowly towards her.

Meg stared. It was Mr Richardson, but in a single night he had become an old man. His eyes were rheumy and red-rimmed and his face had sunk into itself, so that his cheek-bones and chin jutted out and his skin seemed strangely loose. His hair was matted to his head. But most shocking of all was the look he gave her.

'Mr Richardson?' she said again.

But he only turned back to the sea.

The rest of the boat was stirring now, men groaning and muttering, stretching and moving where they could.

In the stern of the boat three men had taken charge. Meg recognised two of them – a young naval officer by the name of Appleby and a steward. The third was a soldier. He didn't look much older than Jim, but he was issuing instructions to the nearest soldiers and they were saluting him. Tins, boxes, blankets, barrels of water, a first-aid box were being passed from man to man and stacked up under a piece of tarpaulin, the steward making notes with a stubby pad and pencil. Meg heard snatches of conversation: about water, and food, and when they'd be rescued. The wounded man was heavy against her and she was so tired, and so cold. She closed her eyes against it all and imagined herself alone again.

'Miss?'

She started. Someone's hand was on her arm.

'Excuse me?' the voice said. He spoke quietly, just to her.

It was Appleby, crouched down beside her. She opened her eyes. His face was very close; she could see the day's growth on his chin. High above him, a couple of seagulls turned.

'I think he's badly wounded,' she said.

'You must come with me,' he said.

'He was moaning in the night, but he's been quiet for a while now.'

'I'm sorry, Miss,' Appleby said. 'But he didn't make it.'

She put a hand to the dead man's cold cheek.

'I didn't even know his name,' she said finally. There was an ache behind her eyes. She didn't want to cry here. She didn't want to be seen to cry.

'You need to come with me,' Appleby said again.

She was puzzled. They were on a lifeboat; there was nowhere to go.

'Come with you where?'

'We've been getting things organised. Supplies, blankets, and so forth. And it's come to our attention that you're the only . . .' He hesitated. 'You're the only female on the boat.'

'Yes.'

'Well . . .'

There was something he'd rather not say. She waited, and after a moment he pressed on. 'As such, as the only female, certain provision needs to be made.'

Meg could feel herself blush.

'So we think, Lieutenant Williams and I, that you'd be more comfortable in the stern. We think it's more suitable.'

Meg kept her eyes down as she followed Appleby but she knew the men were watching her, all of them but Mr Richardson and the dead soldier, laid out now on the boat floor.

'Bad luck at sea,' someone muttered, but loud enough for her to hear. When she looked up, every man but one averted his eyes. Every man but one. Meg stopped and stared.

'Jim!' she mouthed and the man she stared at put his finger to his lips.

She looked away, her heart banging in her chest. He was alive. How had she not seen him before? There he was in the middle of the boat, and when she ventured a second look, she saw that there was a makeshift bandage round his brow and that his uniform was sodden, clinging to him. He must have been one of those rescued from the water in the dark.

'Are you all right?' she mouthed, putting a hand to her head, and she caught his nod before Appleby turned around.

'Miss? Is there a problem?'

She shook her head, and sat down at the back of the boat in her appointed place. Jim was here with her. She couldn't speak to him, and she couldn't touch him, but she could see him. Even out of the corner of her eye she could see him, his bandage like a flag.

The sun rose into a cloudless sky and the day grew warm. Lieutenant Williams gave an order for the men in wet clothes to strip off to vest and trousers and spread their things to dry. Only Mr Richardson refused to do so, and he sat at the end of the boat like a black crow. Meg pinched her eyes nearly shut, so that all she could see were shadows. She used to do that when she was a child. She was one shadow, and her mother was another. Now Mr Richardson was just one shadow, and Jim another, and she was alone on this boat, just like she'd always been.

Crouched on the floor beside her the steward opened a large tin can. Dipping with his thumb and forefinger, he plucked out a peach half. Meg opened her eyes and watched him. His gesture was precise and delicate and small, in the middle of this life-boat in the middle of the ocean, with a dead man on the floor only twenty yards away, and a huge ship sunk, and all these men soaked from the sea and injured, and all of them lost.

With his pocketknife the steward cut the half peach into half again and offered one piece to Meg.

'Breakfast,' he said.

She took it, and turned away so he wouldn't see her tears.

The pieces of peach were passed, one by one, from palm to palm, down the boat. Meg watched and saw Mr Richardson fling his piece to the waves. She watched and saw her lover eat. Then the syrup in the tin can – first to Meg, then the wounded men, then the rest. Again Meg watched, and again she saw her lover drink.

'Just a sip; just a sip,' went like an echo down the boat.

After this there was a ship's biscuit, hard as a brick, with a piece of sardine to wet it, and last of all the beaker of water. Each time the steward served Meg first, and each time she watched Jim eat and drink. She didn't dare try to catch his eye; it was enough that she could see him. Enough that he was alive.

The can was passed back to the steward and Meg watched

him rinse it in the sea and give it to Lieutenant Williams. The lieutenant sat down beside Meg, jigging the peach tin on his knee. He was nervous, she could see that. After a long moment he set it on the floor and leaned in towards her.

'The men are going to use the tin,' he said, pointing to it. He was half-shouting and half-whispering, the wind doing battle with his efforts at discretion.

He paused and she could see that he wanted her to understand something.

'But obviously we need to make separate arrangements for you. So we've earmarked a bucket,' he said, pressing on, 'and we'll hold a piece of canvas around, for your privacy. Might not quite reach, but the men will be ordered to look away. I think you'll find it's fairly private.'

Too much had happened; she felt it in her chest. The journey to marry George, and meeting Jim, and the ship sinking, and seeing people die, and now here on this boat, and Jim and Mr Richardson, and being the only woman. She wished she could wrap herself up and hide, or wriggle down beneath the covers. She needed to be alone. And she didn't know if she could go in that bucket. She just didn't know if she could do it.

'All right?' His voice came to her from a distance and she nodded.

'Will we be rescued?' she said.

'Yes,' he said in the voice of a man who is used to being obeyed.

Meg looked out of the back of the boat while the men passed the tin around. She put her hand in the water. It was cold and dark. She imagined her mother at the kitchen window and George in his desert – the two ends of her journey. Her mother would never get Meg's letter now. And George? She would marry him, if they were rescued, and so she would be safe.

'Miss?' Lieutenant Williams spoke with an air of anticipation. He held out the bucket. 'We're ready for you.'

There was the steward holding the canvas, and all the men – it looked to Meg like every man – every one of them looking at her.

She saw Jim and his face was tender, and Mr Richardson, angry and glaring. She couldn't do it.

'I don't need to,' she said to the lieutenant. 'I'm sorry. Not now,' and she turned back to the water again.

She keeps her eyes wide open. Will says you see better in the dark if you keep your eyes wide open.

Maybe if she goes to sleep, then in the morning he'll be there on his side of the bed and tomorrow they'll go to school and her ma will light the stove and she'll play the morning game with her pa.

'Come back now, Will,' she says, 'no more adventure,' bunching her hands to fists and pushing them under his pillow.

In the bed she lies with her stockings on. Her ma doesn't let her wear them in bed, but there isn't any warm brick and she's cold, and her ma's gone outside calling again. So she keeps the stockings on and puts her cardigan over her nightgown.

If she reaches her hands back behind her, Meg can feel the big brass flower. There's one on her side and one on Will's. Her pa calls them

the bold as brass flowers; he sits on the edge of the bed and makes
the mattress slope and Will shouts and she laughs because Will nearly
falls out. Her pa tells about when he was a boy and how there were five
of them in that same bed, nose to tail to nose to tail to nose.

Will goes to bed after her because he's bigger and sometimes she's
asleep, though she always tries to keep awake. If she does, then they
lie on their backs under the flowers and their feet on the warm bricks
and he tells her facts.

'Facts are true things that you learn,' he tells her. 'Miss Parker says
you can build on things with facts,' and Meg imagines them like bricks
around the bed, one fact on top of the next, and the two of them both
safe inside.

Maybe if she goes to sleep, then he'll be there tomorrow like always.

Meg sang:

> 'Edward Four, Five, Dick the Bad,
> Harrys twain and Ned the lad.
> Mary, Lizzie, James the Vain,
> Charlie, Charlie, James again.

With her face to the waves she sang and sang, holding her
hands over her ears so that all she could hear was her own
voice, and she couldn't think about the lifeboat, or Will, or
anything. And when the boat moved forward suddenly, its first
thrust tipping Meg down towards the water, she only gripped
the boat edge harder and carried on singing to herself. She
was high up on her big bed, waiting for Will, waiting alone.

'Get down, Miss!'

Appleby grabbed her shoulder and pulled her back on to her seat. The boat bucked again and Meg cried out, not because he had hurt her, but because for a moment she had forgotten where she was.

'Nearly had you in the wet,' he said, and she looked at him, not understanding.

'Should make some good ground now,' he said. 'We've got teams organised, turn and turn about. And they're strong lads. It'll keep them fit for fighting.'

There were eight rowers, two on each oar, and with each pull she felt the boat shift.

'We've taken careful bearings, and we reckon we'll make land in seven days, if we aren't picked up first,' Appleby said.

Meg saw that Mr Richardson was sitting only a few feet away now, but when he lifted his head, she thought for a moment it was someone else in his overcoat and with his build, because his face was so changed, yet again, she could barely recognise him. She stared, and he looked right back at her, but she'd swear he didn't see her. His eyes were wide, but he didn't blink, and his mouth was open, as if he were about to shout. He had his arms wrapped about like a straight jacket, and when the boat jolted again, the rowers still finding their stride, he didn't put a hand out to stop himself, but tipped sideways, falling into the soldier beside him.

The soldier pushed him upright, gave him a pat on the back; then Mr Richardson shouted something, his face con-torted, and the soldier half-rose and turned, angry-faced, before checking himself and sitting down again.

'Lost his wife last night, poor man,' the officer said.

'Yes,' she said, and she saw Mrs Richardson standing in the lifeboat and she saw the boat go down.

Meg watched the rowers for a moment, their back and forth – because they had found their stride – a lovely, definite movement in the middle of this endless sea. She envied them their sense of purpose. Also she was cold, despite the sun.

'Could I row?' she said.

Appleby looked at her surprised.

'You'd like to?'

She nodded.

'All right. It's a half hour stretch. We'll put you with Seaman Merrick in the next team,' he said. 'Strongest man on the boat. It'll compensate.'

As she took her place twenty minutes later, she caught Jim's eye; she'd have smiled at him, except that Mr Richardson was staring at her. Though if he knew who she was, he gave no sign of it.

She put her hands on the oar: the wood was smooth, and still warm from the last man. The other seven rowers sat ready, Seaman Merrick beside her, and when the officer gave the order, she pulled with them.

Keeping her eyes on the oar, she paced herself with her neighbour, leaning forward into the motion as he did, then pulling back. At first it was difficult. She got the timing wrong, and the oar jarred against her. But the seaman was steady as a rock and after a few minutes she got the hang of it. Her heart beat harder and she felt the tug in her muscles and the warmth in her hands. They would get there, get there, get there, and George in his desert would be waiting for her; and she would marry him, marry him, marry him and he would put the ring on her finger, and her food on the table, and her babies in her belly, and Will, and Will, and Will . . .

Lean and pull, lean and pull: don't think, don't wish, don't cry.

'Nicely,' she heard the seaman say. 'Nicely for a lady.'

By the time their stint was up Meg was exhausted. Though she was well-used to physical work, her shoulders, back and arms ached, and she'd raised blisters on the palms of her hands. The waves roiled beneath the boat and as she stood, her legs felt unsteady. The next group of rowers was ready and she followed Seaman Merrick off the bench. She noticed Mr Richardson moving forward to take his place and she thought him very brave.

'Well done,' someone said to her, and some of the men applauded. When she caught Jim's eye, he winked at her and she couldn't stop a small smile. Already the next men were seated at their oars and she turned to clamber her way back.

The blow laid Meg to the floor, a fist punched in between her shoulder blades, robbing her of air, crunching her ribs. She fell and a voice followed her down, spitting words like shrapnel.

'Bitch! Whore! I saw you making eyes. You should be dead.'

He was on top of her, his hands at her throat, and she was choking, she couldn't breathe, her head pressed against the floor. There were shouts and the boards shifted and creaked, but the voice went on like poison in her ear.

'My wife dead! It should be you. You in that boat. You drowned!'

Then someone else was shouting, and the lifeboat rocked, catching the waves broadside with a hard slap sound that banged through her head. But he was doing more than shouting; he was roaring and Meg knew his voice because she had heard it raised once before. Only now Jim roared with rage.

She felt Mr Richardson's fingers pulled away from her neck and his weight yanked off her. And when she opened her eyes there was Jim with his fist raised.

'Don't,' she said, and all her fear was carried in the cry. Fear for her life in this war, in this lifeboat; fear because she desired the man she couldn't marry, and she would marry the man she didn't desire.

He looked at her, wild-eyed, as mad to see as Mr Richardson.

'No!' she shouted.

She shook her head. She was so weary. There was too much to hold in and she couldn't do it any more.

Slowly Jim lowered his fist. Meg closed her eyes and imagined herself at home and alone in her bed. She was small again and the bed was her castle. She imagined the covers pulled high and tucked in, and sleeping beside her, turned away into the crook of his dream, was Will. He was there, and just for a moment she let go, and it felt so good, so warm and reassuring.

It was no more than a few seconds, no more than that.

Nothing had changed when she opened her eyes. Jim still stood over Mr Richardson, and the rowers still watched. But she felt the warmth between her legs, and the wetness.

'Please God, no!' she said, and the oars dipped and the boat went on.

EARTH

The view from the house was one of the best. Everybody said so. Everybody said how lucky they'd been, what with this view, and the pond, and the air and the trees. Even the earth they were lucky with, apparently; the black soil that grew things either very big or very small.

The farm had belonged to a German couple and they'd sold the house to George for a song. So he told her, anyway. Sold it and run, he didn't know where. North Africa, probably. The land had gone to the Bromleys, a nice addition to their coffee plantation, and George and Meg had got the house and the garden around. Lock, stock and barrel, everything: furniture, glassware, linen, rugs, right down to the books, all in German, and a rheumy old dog called Otto, who would come running to the right tone of voice, whatever you called him, little Will discovered.

Lying in bed Meg would run her fingers over the pillow-case till she felt the raised edge of the monogram: 'KvG'. She was sleeping on someone else's name, and sometimes she was sure, even now, that she dreamed someone else's dreams.

Back in their first married months in Kenya, George and Meg had lived in Kandula, the town, in the little bungalow he had inherited from his predecessor.

'Reggie Crumlin was single,' George said, 'and from what

I've gathered, not very interested in anything except whisky and big game. And by the time he retired, it was only whisky.'

Meg thought that Reggie Crumlin had certainly not been interested in the house, which had little in the way of furniture, not even a good bed, and only two chairs. It was, besides, too small for the two of them and with their first baby on the way so very quickly, George had jumped at the chance of the house in the hills, where the air was clearer and there was room for a nursery and the red dust didn't lie quite so deep in the months before the long rains. They could entertain more easily now, he said, and he felt happier with Meg here, when he had to be away. It was safer, especially with Sita now sleeping in the next room and Yusuf only a shout away from the front door.

'You're sure we can afford it?' Meg had said, and was answered with a curt nod. If that was all he would say, then she knew she'd get no more from him and there was no point fretting. It was usual for a husband to take care of financial matters. Other women spoke of their difficulties with this, but none did any differently. But Meg still wondered how they could afford it, because his salary was modest and he had no money behind him any more than she did.

This early, the air was still cold and Meg shivered and wrapped her gown around her more tightly. But she didn't go in because she liked it, when the mist still hung in the hills and the colours were less fierce. Sometimes in the early morning, the hills weren't there. They could come and go so fast, it was like magic. As if a magician with a flourish had flung his silky scarf and made them disappear, and flung it again and there they were. She had seen such a thing once when Mrs Rogers hired a magician for the Christmas party. He'd stood with his hat and cape in one of the vicarage rooms and done his tricks before the village children. She remembered the feeling very well; she'd liked it, being tricked, because she knew he had the rabbit safe somewhere, so she didn't mind not knowing where. Maybe that was how she felt about George and the money. She didn't mind too much not knowing because she trusted him to keep things safe. They had been married for five years now and he had reliably been everything she had needed him to be.

A voice at her shoulder. Yusuf, the house boy, stood with a tray.

'Tea, Memsaab.' He placed it on the table. 'Master William is awake,' he said.

Meg never announced herself to Yusuf in the morning but somehow he always knew when she was up and he would be there on the veranda with a tray of tea never more than ten minutes after she had stepped out.

'Thank you,' she said.

The tea drew a thin, warm line down her insides, down to her belly. Soon Will would run to find her, and Sita would bring the baby, and there would be breakfast and things to decide, meals, and the diary to run through, because her memory had been terrible since the baby and she couldn't remember, otherwise, what she should be doing or where she should be going. But just for now she stood on the veranda and looked out.

George was in the north, beyond the hills, supervising a crop scheme – he had told her what it was, but she couldn't remember the details. Something to do with ground nuts, she thought, or perhaps tobacco. They were waiting on the rains. Everybody was waiting on the rains. Then there were two *barazas* to attend, and he had several cases to hear, mostly land disputes, he said, and a whole list of other things. He had been away nearly a week and when he returned tomorrow, he would be filthy with dust and bone tired and he would want the house and the garden and Meg to be just so. She understood; she didn't mind. He worked very hard. It was only that she seemed to be so tired, too, and everything was such a tremendous effort.

Somewhere inside there were the sounds of doors opening and closing and a child's voice. She took another look across the valley, as if to take in the view, breathe it in and hold it there, like a lungful of smoke; as if she could suck it into her blood this way, even though it was the wrong landscape really because she already had a place that lived inside her.

Other people saw animals in this view from the house. George had pointed out antelope – eland he told her, the biggest kind – grazing on the plain, and different birds, and once a shadow in the hills that was a pair of lions. He saw them with binoculars. About the lions Meg had nodded – she believed him – but she didn't want to see them.

She'd had a letter from her mother that week, telling her all sorts from home: how much things cost now, and how long spring was taking to arrive; and how hard getting about was, what with her legs, and now her hands were sore as well. Meg was accustomed to this. Ever since she'd left, her mother had painted the price each month in her letters. Meg had got used to it, and anyway she'd felt less guilty since the children were born. In return she wrote chatty letters that were sorry for the sore hands and the slow spring. Then she wrote all sorts about the children, and George, and she told her mother gossip and how the Natives lived. These days her letters were wrapped around a post office money order.

The only person Meg didn't talk about was herself. She never said that she still missed her father; or that she still looked for her brother, though less fiercely now. And she never told her mother how much she missed things: the bed with its bold as brass flowers, and the raised pavement she'd walked to school along every day, and the church with its stained glass, the fields, and the woods where the boys went to play. Because though she'd left and travelled to another continent, these were the places that inhabited her mind.

'Boo!'

Small hands gripped her calves and she felt her son's head butt against her legs.

'Boo!' he said again.

His fingers were like so many little pebbles, pressing and ticklish. Bending and turning in one movement, she picked him up and kissed him, once on each cheek, and he squealed his pleasure and threw his head this way and that. It was harder, doing this, than it had been even the few months back when she was very pregnant, but she would not let it go. Will sat on her hips, legs wrapped around her middle and it was her turn to butt her head.

'My blue-eyed boy,' she murmured, and she buried her face in him till he wriggled to be let down.

She set him on the ground again. He had a little boy's, not a baby's body now, not an ounce of fat on him, and as if by way of consolation to herself, she patted his head to feel his soft hair.

'Go and tell Kibaki we'll have breakfast,' she said.

'But I'm still in my pyjamas.'

'No matter.'

She went to the nursery and found Sita feeding the baby. He was a hungry baby with eyes only for his bottle, and when it was empty and Meg took him to her shoulder to wind him, he grizzled a little.

'We're having breakfast,' Meg said. 'Will you get him dressed?'

She kissed the top of his head and gave him back to Sita.

'I can still feel it,' she said, putting an arm across her breasts.

'He needs stronger food now,' Sita said. 'More than milk.'

Will had little interest in food and he sat on his cushion at the dining table with his elbows planted, napkin tucked into his pyjama shirt, toying with the squares of toast and the slices of orange that Kibaki had arranged for him.

'I want to play,' Will said.

'When you've eaten your breakfast and drunk your milk.' Meg nudged one of the toast squares. 'Kibaki has made a pretty flower this morning.'

'It's not a flower, it's a star.'

This was one of their jokes, Kibaki's toast. Sometimes he cut it into circles and sometimes he made a face out of the different shapes. Today he had made a star, or flower, out of the lozenge-shaped pieces. When Will began, finally, to eat a piece, it was Kibaki's job to pretend to be upset by the disarranging.

Meg sipped her tea. The china, left by the fled Germans, was delicate. The tea service was pale blue in colour, decorated with a frieze of tiny flowers. She almost thought she could see the light through the side of the tea cup, and she took care, lifting it and setting it back down.

'Eat up, Will.'

The little boy traced around the flowers on his plate in a half-absent, half-provocative way.

'I want to play,' he said.

'If you don't eat up your toast, you'll have a little boy's plate again tomorrow,' Meg said, 'and I'll have to tell Daddy when he comes home.'

Will ate a mouthful of toast, chewing laboriously, and rearranged the star shape, making the space between the toast points equal to his eye.

Yusuf came in, walking across the polished boards with his long, delicate stride. He was like a crane high-stepping in the shallows, all knee and angle. Will watched him from beneath his eyelids. Yusuf set a dish on the sideboard: 'Eggs, memsaab, and your diary.' Placing the diary on the table beside Meg, he turned to go out.

Will pushed a piece of toast to and fro.

'Anyway Yusuf's my real daddy. Cos he doesn't ever eat anything either, and he's skinny like me,' he said.

Meg had never seen Yusuf's calm broken – not when the rains failed, nor when thieves took his best cow; not even when his own child, his daughter Jata, was so ill they feared for her life and drove her in the Austin in the dead of night through the hills to the mission hospital, Yusuf at the wheel, silent and focussed, pushing the little car to its limits.

But now she saw his back stiffen, and when he turned, there was panic on his face.

Meg had listened to the gossip amongst the women at the club, and she'd overheard the men talking over the port right here in her dining room. It was absurd, to be worried about a small boy's words like this, but Africans had been attacked, left for dead, for little more. All it would take would be Will repeating this to one of his little toto friends and next thing Yusuf might be beaten to a pulp with his own panga, like the African they'd mentioned at the club who gave a piggyback to his boss's child.

Meg laughed. She heard the sound as if it came from outside herself.

'Don't be silly, Will. Yusuf has his own son, and his own daughter, you know that. And you are mine. Mine and your daddy's.'

'George Lombard Garrowby,' Will said, like a lesson learned.

'Memsaab?' Yusuf said.

'Thank you, Yusuf.'

Meg waited till she was sure he was gone before speaking.

'If you eat up all your toast then I'll tell you the story about when I got married to your daddy.'

'Before I was born,' Will said.

'Eat up your toast.'

'Before I was a twinkle,' he said.

'Yes.'

'Properly tell it?'

She nodded.

So Will ate the toast as if it were the simplest thing in the world, and Meg began. She didn't try to abridge the story or amend it. He had a child's sharp ear for being short-changed and he would only have stopped eating and made her go back. She told him about how she had travelled across the huge ocean to marry his father, and how George travelled across the great desert to marry her; and how he carried her wedding ring with him in its special box.

'And then he waited and waited by the sea for me to arrive, and the boat didn't come and the boat didn't come, and everybody else that was waiting, one by one, they went home.'

'Tell it how they went,' Will said, 'all the different people,' because he had heard this story before and he wanted it told just so.

'Well, there were the soldiers, and the vicar, and the motorcar with the dog inside . . .'

'And the man with the white hat, and it was a proper dog, not a pye dog,' Will said, his mouth still full.

'Yes, a proper dog with a collar round its neck that put its head out of the motor car window. But they all went home when the boat didn't come . . .'

Will bounced in his seat and broke in with his own recitation, because this story was part of the family rosary: ' . . . First of all the dog and the mummy and daddy and the two big girls went home, and then the soldiers went home, and the man with the white hat and last of all the vicar but . . .' He shook his head slowly from side to side. ' . . . not Daddy.'

'No, not Daddy. And when the boat finally arrived, and everybody was so thirsty and dirty, and hungry . . .'

' . . .and you were so dirty cos you hadn't cleaned your face with a flannel not for days and so hungry you would eat a horse . . .'

'I was so dirty and so thirsty and tired and hungry, and who was standing there, waiting?'

Will nodded slowly, solemnly, like a boy beyond his years. Absentmindedly he put the last finger of toast in his mouth.

'It was Daddy, and he showed you the ring, and the next day the vicar who had gone away married you in his church.'

Almost it had happened like that. Almost. Meg touched the ring. They had predicted seven, but it was eleven days at sea in the lifeboat before they were rescued. She couldn't properly remember the last of them.

A ship found them drifting, and when they took her off the lifeboat, they said all she asked for, again and again, was a clean dress. They thought it funny, and a product of her delirium. Her skin was burned from the sun, she was feverish with sunstroke, she had lost nearly two stone in weight and what she longed for, the only thing, was a clean dress. This the men approved of. This was a mark of her will to live and when the captain of the rescue ship gave her away less than a week later, in a clean and borrowed frock, he told her that a young woman like her, with such a spirit, deserved this marriage and he was sure her father would be proud when he knew.

She remembered just a single figure standing when the ship came into port. Just a single, solitary figure waiting patiently, an act of faith in the midst of so much bad faith. It was like a scene from a novel and ever after it stayed this way in her mind, though later she thought her memory had surely played tricks, because there must have been a horde of people swarming about the quayside, not just the single one. He stood still and held a small box in his hand, though till she was nearly up to him, it looked like his fist clenched. And when he saw her, a little figure decked out in a pair of sailor's ducks, he just raised his arm, as though he had expected her to arrive like this. And before he greeted her, he held the box out on the palm of his hand, ceremonious, and flipped it open so that the ring caught the sun, making a hard line of light.

'But what nearly happened to the ring?' Meg said. She wanted to hurry through this part of the tale this morning, but Will was a stickler and she'd given her word.

'It slipped off,' Will said, 'cos it was so loose, only Daddy saw it slip and he picked it up.'

It had been so loose on her finger, she feared it would drop and be lost in the dust; so she wore it on a chain around her neck for a month, trying it on each day for size, till gradually, as her weight and her figure returned, she grew into it again.

'We were so long in the little boat that we nearly ran out of food,' Meg said.

'And water. Tell about the water, and the funny man who drank the sea, and the kind one with the hurt head who said he'd walk you home.'

She looked at Will, his eager face. The man was called Jim, but she never said his name aloud when she told the story. So to Will he was simply the man with the hurt head. He'd eaten every last bit of toast, but she couldn't tell any more.

'Enough,' she said. 'Maybe later,' and she rang the bell. 'Please tell Sita that we'll start Henry on some ground rice,' she said when Yusuf came in.

'That's only baby food,' Will said.

'And Henry is only a baby. But he'll be eating his breakfast faster than you very quickly, and then who will get more stories?'

She pulled Will's chair out from the table and tipped it forward so that he slid, giggling, to the floor.

'Can't you even sit on a chair yet?' she said, giving him her hands and jumping him to his feet. 'I am going to look at my diary now and you are going with Yusuf to find Sita and get dressed.'

'Don't want to get dressed,' Will said, crossing his arms in defiance.

She couldn't resist a last touch, putting her hands around his middle, slipping them under his pyjama jacket to feel his warm skin.

'Go on,' she said, pushing him gently, and he went, only just remembering to throw his mother a sulky look as he left the room.

Although the house was still cool, outside the sun shone with the ferocity Meg knew now to come before the rains. Everything was coloured in ochres – reds and oranges and browns – everything drawn in, sucked dry, waiting for the rains to start.

Meg sat on at the table, the diary open. Like all the rooms in the house, the dining room still felt like someone else's: the ghosts of the departed Germans still sat in the chairs, still looked out from the windows. But despite them, Meg liked this room best in the house. There was room to breathe here and she felt nearly at ease. Or as at ease as she would any-where, in a country, amongst a people, mixing in a class not her own, and married to a man she was grateful to, but didn't love.

On the mahogany sideboard she set fresh flowers daily, a great, untidy vase full, cut from the garden she had made, and the rich, dark wood took in and gave back their colours in its shiny surface. Broad windows and French doors opened out onto the veranda, and beyond she could see the hills, with clouds above like false promises. The sun never shone in directly but the room seemed to gather up the light even so. Sometimes she set the ceiling fan turning, not so much because it was too warm, because in that room it was rarely too warm, but because it seemed exotic, and because she found the slow, steady turn of the blades restful, and she would sit, with her elbows on the starched white cloth, and let her eyes close.

Soon she would go down into the town and do her errands, then an engagement for lunch. In the afternoon she had promised herself an hour in her garden while the children rested. The evening Meg had to herself and she held the time in mind like a gift to be opened later. It should be a nice day.

Over the last four years Meg had learned well how to be as a member of the British middle class and as a colonial wife, and on a number of occasions the second task had worked as a convenient mask for her mistakes with the first. Other wives understood her confusion over how to order groceries because they'd all had to learn how to treat the watu.

'Speak clearly to them and remember they're not so much devious as simple,' Mrs Bromley had advised.

And when the soup spoons were in the wrong position, her guests laughed at the crude ways of the Somali houseboy, who probably ate with his fingers at home so couldn't be expected to know any better; and Meg, to her shame, because it was she who had placed the spoons, laughed with them.

In the kitchen Meg spoke with Kibaki and wrote out the list into her notebook. George had showed her how to set it out in their first month of marriage and there was a line of notebooks in his desk, every penny Meg had spent in the last five years listed and totalled. He liked to have control of things – she'd learned that very well – and he didn't like surprises.

That's why he'd still been waiting for her ship to come in, as if he could compel it, and her, to do the proper thing, the expected thing, just by not believing otherwise. Afterwards, when he told the story to somebody, he told it as though it were somehow her fault that he had to wait so long and it was so dusty and hot and he couldn't take a bath.

'It is Mr Garrowby's last night away, and we'll all have boiled eggs tonight,' Meg said to Kibaki, 'and I'll cook them. Yusuf is back then, so you may go home at five.'

She turned to go out and then remembered.

'How is your daughter?'

Kibaki nodded.

'She is still not well, Memsaab,' he said.

'I'm sorry,' Meg said, and she felt her old blush rise. She'd rarely been down to the African lines, although they were only just beyond the garden, and never into an African hut. So she didn't know what kind of place Kibaki and his family lived in; though she knew, from other women, that the African hut was called a rondavel. She'd seen them from outside, of course: clusters of circular thatched huts with little squares of land attached dotted with colour, where they grew their food, and always crowds of little, naked totos running about. From a distance it all looked very lively and what Mrs Richardson had described once, telling Meg about Africa, as *au naturel*, which Meg had taken to understand as quite in the natural order of things. But she did wonder what kind of sanitation there was and whether the children went to school at all, and she couldn't help noticing that the totos they passed in the motor car usually had big bellies and dirty faces.

And seen closer up, the little boys Will played with had crusty eyes and snotty noses, though she couldn't be sure they were the same boys each time. She had wiped Will's hands and face with a solution of TCP the first time, but after that she hadn't worried so much. Though she hadn't told George about these boys, and she had tried to impress on Will that it would be better to keep the game a secret.

'The Africans don't want to live like us,' George reassured her. 'God knows, we've asked them. Don't trust our doctoring, don't like our farming methods. So live and let live, I say.'

Meg knew there were other views about this; there were quite heated discussions amongst the wives sometimes when they met for coffee. But most of the people she had met, people George assured her were good types, thought as he did. And it was true, after all, that George himself spent much of his time helping Africans as best he could.

So Meg didn't ask Kibaki any more about his daughter – such as what the matter was, or if she could help – because in an emergency she believed he would ask her for help, and otherwise she thought he would rather she kept out.

'Will was very pleased with his star,' she said. 'He ate it nearly all up.'

'Thank you, Memsaab.'

Again Kibaki gave his short bow – she often heard him teasing Will, but he was always serious with her – and she went to find Yusuf.

When Meg left the house, when she left the hills: those were the times that she felt as if she belonged in them, and this morning she'd have been more than happy to stay up there.

But there was shopping to be done and she must go into the town. So Yusuf drove the Austin down towards Kandula, the small, mosquito-ridden town eight miles away, and Meg tried to put away her mood.

They drove in towards the main street – past the railway depot and the string of dukas and shanty beer parlours, then the Sports Club, where the Union Jack hung from its flag like old washing, and the Leicester Hotel. And though she didn't remember much from her time living there now, the feeling that surfaced was an old familiar. It was like the chill in the stomach she got as a child when her mother found her out in a lie and it lay over her spirits, soft and penetrating, like the deep, red dust that lay over the streets before the rains turned it to mud.

In an effort to shake it, she asked Yusuf about his family: a sister married and gone to live in Nairobi, his widowed mother, his brother. She asked after each of his wives: 'Is Amina well? And Faisa?'

And after each enquiry he bowed his head so that his turban brushed against the windscreen, and said: 'She is, I thank you.'

Only about his brother would he say a little more: 'He has travelled to Nakuru with a herd of cattle because a man there has named a good price,' he said.

'Your brother is a good trader,' Meg said.

'He is a good Somali,' Yusuf said. 'You are accepting if I take my leave this afternoon?'

'Yes,' Meg said. 'You'll be back by five?'

He nodded, but offered no further conversational distraction and the two of them fell quickly into their habitual silence. Usually Meg liked this; there was something restful and companionable in it. But today she wished she had a European at the wheel who would gossip, and chat about the weather, and take her mind off things. If she could have thought of a reason, she'd have ordered Yusuf to turn around and drive back home.

The breeze that blew through the hills had given up before it reached the plain and the heat in the town was damp and oppressive. Meg left her grocery list with Mr Gupta and sent Yusuf to the African market to buy meat and cassava. George liked to see only English food on his table, but Sita had discovered that Will would eat cassava with some sugar added when he would eat nothing else. If Yusuf could find some mangoes, even better. She walked along the street, her mind still half caught in the past, still remembering the day she arrived in Africa and the truths she had told Will this morning, and the lies.

Meg bought stamps in the post office, exchanging the necessary courtesies with Mrs Grant: 'Thank you, yes, it's very close; yes, let's hope the rains come soon, yes.'

But she didn't check for letters because she hadn't yet replied to Alice's and she'd only just had one from her mother. So she was on her way out, nearly gone, when Mrs Grant called to her.

'Mrs Garrowby, you've got a letter.'

Meg stopped and turned to the wall of mailboxes. She had done this so often in the last years, hoping against hope. What if he had found out where she was? What if he wrote to her? It was only in the last year, since being pregnant with Henry, that she had let go, or nearly let go, of this hope and now here she was, heart racing, not knowing what to wish for.

She slipped her hand into the box: a single, flimsy airmail letter, and when she looked at the handwriting, she felt the disappointment, despite herself. There was her mother's hand, the address looking a little scrawled, more carelessly written than usual, as if done in a hurry, though that might just be because Meg was looking at it more closely than usual. She turned the letter over, but there was nothing unusual to see. Why had she written again? Her mother was a creature of strict habits, obsessive even, and she wrote to Meg once a month, never more and never less, on the first day of the month. That letter had arrived less than a week ago.

'Nothing you weren't looking for?' Mrs Grant said.

'No,' Meg said, but already something was rising in her that she needed to put away.

She left the post office and stood on the dusty street, the letter in her hand. Then, decided, she put it in her bag. She would open it later, not now. Later, when she was on her own and she had more time. Because after all she didn't mind not knowing what it said, yet. Because after all she had spent a lifetime, nearly, not knowing things. It was a familiar feeling, and she didn't need to rush away from it.

Mr Gupta had her groceries ready by the time she returned, and Yusuf was waiting too, holding two long sweet cassava roots for Will in one hand and in the other, the meat, wrapped up in newspaper and tied with a piece of string, held away from his body, away from his crisp overshirt and sarong. Blood was already soaking through the cricket news and the flies were thick. Meg thought of England and the butcher's shop in the village with its cold, white tiles and scrubbed wooden benches. She thought of the small, tidy pieces of meat that were all she and her mother could afford.

'Let's go home,' she said.

The drive to the house curved round past the Bromleys' coffee sheds and up between two groves of eucalyptus that bowed, graceful as Masai, in the wind. There was no roasting going on now, but Meg could always smell, or fancied she could, the smoky, woody smell of the roasting beans. As ever, a cluster of children appeared on the verges and ran beside the motor car, some with a hand to its hot metal flank, some carrying a smaller child on their hip. Most were naked or wearing just a rough shirt, and all were barefoot. Anticipating Meg's request, Yusuf brought the motor car to near walking pace and the car grumbled slowly up to the house.

Meg climbed out. Will would be here any second in his short trousers and buttoned shirt, and his sandals against the jiggas and broad-brimmed hat that George had given him so he could pretend to be on safari, running out to see what she'd brought, to see if there was anything exciting, Sita behind him, half-running to keep up.

Yusuf took the meat from the boot and Meg waited. She felt in her bag for the letter. A butterfly fluttered in her chest. Perhaps her mother had decided to visit, after all; or perhaps she had fallen ill, or come into something unexpected. Money, or love.

'Did you see Will?' Meg said when Yusuf returned for the groceries.

'No, Memsaab.'

'Or Sita?'

'No, Memsaab. I am leaving now till teatime?'

'Yes,' she said, nodding absently. 'Of course.'

Everything was quiet – no small boy sounds. She opened the front door. It was heavy, resistant, built by the Germans to withstand . . . She didn't know what it was built to withstand. Masai spears, perhaps.

'Will?' she called. 'Sita?'

She looked for him in the drawing room – behind the sofas, under the low table, behind the door, the curtains. There was some paper and colouring pencils on the table and a picture with green and red lines and a circle that might be a face. The lines were so definite, as if Will knew in his mind's eye exactly what he wanted to set down. She loved to watch him drawing. There was no hesitation in it and he always knew when it was finished.

There was no one in the dining room, or in the kitchen, so she turned and walked along the corridor to the bedroom Will shared with Henry. She didn't think he would be in here because he wasn't allowed when Henry had his sleep, and Sita would have removed him. She thought that if Will was nowhere else, then he would be with Sita, surely. Quietly she opened the bedroom door. It was dark inside.

'Will?' she called softly.

In the half dark she saw a figure seated on the bed and when she came closer, she saw that it was Sita and that she had Henry on her lap.

'What is it?' Meg said quietly, putting a hand to Henry's forehead. It was hot. He looked up at her with heavy eyes, with the weary, disinterested look of the feverish.

'Soon after you left for Kandula,' Sita said. 'He is exhausted now, but at first I could not calm him.'

Sitting on the bed, Meg stroked his brow. His soft baby hair was plastered to his head.

'Has he been sick?'

'Only crying, and very hot.'

'Not floppy, or jerky?' She mimed what she meant, to be sure. 'You've checked for a rash?' she said, lifting Henry's vest. Sita nodded.

'And he's happy being held?'

'Yes. He has been calmer since I closed the curtains.'

'Then for now we must just wait and see. I will send Yusuf for the doctor if he is no better by the evening. Where is Will?'

'He is in the drawing room with his paper and his pencils.'

Meg shook her head.

'He's not.'

'But I told him to stay there till you returned. A good boy,' Sita said.

'I don't think he's in the house, or the garden,' Meg said.

'I told him because Henry, he was not well and so Will must stay there.'

'He would have come when he heard the motor car,' Meg said. 'He always comes running then, in case it is his father.'

'He is perhaps hide and seeking?' Sita said.

'Yes,' Meg said. 'Yes. Perhaps that's it. I'll go and hunt for him; Kibaki is making a cake later, for Mr Garrowby's return tomorrow. I'll promise him cake if he will come out. Kibaki can make him a cupcake for tea today. He always comes out for cake.'

So she called for him through the house and then through the garden, but there was no sign of him and no sound. He wasn't there. Perhaps he had quite forgotten Sita's instruction and run off to play. But he'd soon come back, not because he was hungry – he never seemed to be hungry – but because he had remembered that his mother was returning from the town, or because Kibaki had promised to let him whip the egg whites.

She was not out of breath but her heart was thumping in her chest and she felt a sweat break on her skin.

'Will!' she called out, the sound like a bell note in the sharpening air.

The valley and those beautiful hills were full of dangers, full of her fears, and they held no mercy for her little boy. The lions and snakes would be prowling and slithering. There were thorns and wild pig holes and all manner of things that could hurt him.

There was never any mercy for little boys, she thought.

She tried to think calmly. Tried to think what George would do. Perhaps she should go back to the house and up to George's study. You could see further from up there; you could see things that were invisible from the lawn. Or should she walk down the drive, now, hunt for him? She'd take one of the sticks from the hall stand to beat things back with. Because Will might have gone that way; he might have gone further than he ought, looking out for her and Yusuf, or running after something, or someone. Perhaps he had fallen and hurt himself; or perhaps he was trapped . . .

She looked down beyond the lawn. Sita should go and look, not her. Sita was better at looking – it was her country, after all – and Meg should stay with Henry. It wasn't meningitis, Meg was sure of that. Nor yellow fever. Mrs Pritchard's girls had all got yellow fever in the last rains, but it hadn't been too bad, she had said, not so different from the usual.

Meg knew what to do for Henry. These fevers that took the children: if it wasn't malaria, then usually they ran their course quite quickly, and all you could do was keep the child cool, and give them water, and comfort them. Will had been ill a few times. So far none of them had caught malaria, but she supposed it would only be a matter of time, if they stayed in Africa, despite her efforts with the chloroquine.

She walked down the middle of the drive. Safest place, they said. Nothing going to creep up on you, or slither out, or nip you without a warning at least, if you walked in the middle of your drive. It turned, a graceful, sweeping arc, and she was out of sight of the house, walking still between the high eucalyptus trees. George said the Germans had done well, planting so many of these, because they drained the soil and discouraged mosquitoes. She liked them, with their high branches and their airy shade and the bark hanging in rips and tears.

'William,' she called out between the trees. 'Will.'

She should go back and send Sita to look for him. Sita knew his hiding places; she knew where the children went. Besides, Meg was anxious about Henry. She wanted to see for herself that his skin was clear, that he wasn't floppy, or stiff. It wasn't that she didn't believe Sita, but he was her baby.

'Will!' she called.

She was out of sight of the house now. Perhaps she should go to the African lines. She'd never been on her own before, and she wasn't sure what she would say. Sita, or George, usually did the talking and she just smiled a lot. But this time she had lost Will, so she supposed that's all she needed to say. And it didn't matter what they thought. It didn't matter at all.

She always felt embarrassed standing in their village, that was the point. They seemed to do so much outside their huts; they lived more or less in full view of everybody else and she felt as though she'd walked into somebody else's house without an invitation. Imagine if she were to do that at home. Her mother didn't go into anybody else's house, ever, and Meg had always been careful to make sure she was properly invited; even by the Gilmers, who loved her, and by Mrs Gregg, Alice's mother, who had known Meg since she was in the infant class. The Africans were always very welcoming, very friendly, at least to Meg's face, but she knew there was something important that she didn't understand at all about them.

Anyway, if Will had wandered down there, they'd have brought him back by now. Little Bwana, they called him.

'My little bwana,' she said to herself, and she remembered her last touch of him at breakfast that morning, how much of a little boy he was now, so slight and lean, and the last softness of his baby body gone.

She stopped at the bottom of the drive. In all the last four years, she'd never walked beyond here. She felt faint and her throat was tight, as if there were something she couldn't swallow, and she crouched down, hands on either side for balance, in the dust. A memory came of snow and she shook her head to clear it. After a minute she stood up again and turned to walk back. The strength had gone from her legs and every step was an effort, as though she had been walking for hours.

'Will,' she called out, but her voice was weak. He'd only hear if he were very close by.

When she heard the children, she heard them quite clearly, more than one of them, laughing or calling out. But they were too far off for her to tell whether one of the voices was Will's. She scrambled up the bank into the grove of trees, her breath so loud in her ears that she kept stopping and holding it so as to hear the children's sounds again, then setting off once more. After a couple of minutes she found them: four little totos, one of them Will.

From where she stood, the children couldn't see her and so she watched, unseen, and waited for her heart to slow down and her breath to be steadier. They were running to and fro, calling out, playing in a clearing between the trees where the sun broke through and streaked the air. One of the children was a girl and she held a tin bowl Meg recognised from the kitchen. The others waved sticks like spears. She watched Will raise his stick above his head and stamp his feet and she heard him shout 'Row Row', and throw back his head. Then the two African boys joined in and they shouted something out in unison that, whatever it was, wasn't English. Whatever it was, it sounded wild and strange. She saw in her mind's eye the picture she'd found in the drawing room with its red and blue lines striking away from the circle. She had guessed it as a person with a head and limbs; but watching her son now she didn't know what it was, and she thought how much of a stranger he remained. She couldn't imagine how it must feel to be him. A wash of pleasure ran over her to see her small son standing so separately, playing without fear. She had been very frightened by his disappearance and she would have to be cross with him in a minute, but for now she was glad that he could run around fearless like this.

She stepped out into the children's game, appearing, as if like magic, from between the trees, and the African children turned tail and fled, soundlessly, vanished in moments, so that Will stood deserted in the middle of the clearing, a little, grubby European boy with a stick in one hand and the tin bowl somehow in the other. Meg smiled. He looked so left alone.

Will didn't look at Meg, only lifted his chin and planted his stick more firmly in the ground, still king, or hunter, or warrior, or whatever it was he was playing at. She felt heavy with relief and she wanted most of all to pick him up and hug him to her. But she put on her severest voice.

'William,' she said. 'Sita told you to stay in the drawing room.'

Will looked down at the ground, his jaw stubborn.

'She told you to stay there till I returned. When I came back, I couldn't find you and I've been very worried. Why did you disobey her?'

He shrugged.

'I thought you might be hurt. I didn't know what had happened to you,' she said. She waited again.

'William?' she said.

'Njombo called to me,' he muttered finally, still staring at the ground.

'Njombo?'

'He knocked first,' Will said. 'He invited me.'

'He knocked where?'

'On the window. I was drawing my picture and he put his hand on the window, and he invited me.'

He made a beckoning gesture with his hand to show how it had been, as if that explained it.

'Njombo is the toto you have played with before?' Meg said.

'His father is a chief,' Will said.

'But Njombo is only a little boy, like you. You must ask me

before you go to play with him.'

She put her fingers under his chin and lifted his head.

'Look at me, Will.'

He didn't want to meet her eye and he looked one way and then the other.

'Njombo's not the same as you,' she said. 'He comes from here. He's an African. This is his country, his home . . .'

Will broke in, his voice impassioned.

'But it's mine too.'

Meg shook her head.

'No. Not so that you can play like Njombo plays. You're an English boy. One day we'll go home to England and then you can play like this. You'll be a bigger boy then, too, and I won't need to run and find you.'

Will crossed his arms and stamped his foot on the ground. Meg smiled. George crossed his arms when he was angry, and for a second Will was a miniature George. She took his grimy, reluctant hand and tugged him back through the trees towards the drive.

Mrs Bromley tsked through her teeth and mixed another gin and orange squash. She pointed to Meg's glass.

'No, thank you,' Meg said, 'else I'll be asleep this afternoon.'

'Nothing wrong with that,' Mrs Bromley said.

'No, but I've promised myself an hour in the garden.'

'Anyway . . .' Mrs Bromley said.

She settled herself in her chair and Meg waited. Mrs

Bromley always took her time. She was a large, comfortable woman in a large, comfortable floral print dress. Indeed Meg had never seen her in anything except floral prints and she had even wondered aloud to George recently whether one of Mrs Bromley's ways of keeping England about her was to walk around in a perpetually flowering garden.

Meg looked across the drawing room. Mrs Bromley's furniture, too, was upholstered in flowers, and now swathes of bias-cut dahlias rustled and shifted themselves dizzyingly upon a bank of upholstered marigolds and daisies.

What do I do, Meg wondered, to keep England about me? It isn't dressing in flowers. But it might be growing them. I used to like putting them in jars when I was little.

Mrs Bromley was in the middle of a lecture.

'. . . the thing is,' she said, 'everybody is an immigrant. Us, the Masai, Kikuyu, everybody. It's the Arabs who've been here the longest. Mr Bromley said thousands of years, but I'm not sure I believe that. The Arabs are the kings of trade, of course; while the Masai and the Kikuyu just wander about with spears and count their cows and goats. Don't really grow very much, only what they need. You can see that in their shambas, can't you?'

Meg remembered a line of jam jars on the kitchen table once, and one dandelion, was it? Or some other pretty weed, in each. Her mother hadn't thought them pretty, though. She wondered whether her mother picked flowers for the table, now she'd gone. Her mother did most things at the kitchen table. She'd have written the letter there. The most recent, unexpected letter. Maybe she put daffodils in a jar. It was that time of year in England.

'Can't you?' Mrs Bromley repeated.

Meg nodded. 'Of course,' she said, and Mrs Bromley looked at her for a moment, then went on.

'Then there are the Europeans. We might be the newest, but we do know about farming. So we've got on and bought the land, fair and square, planted the coffee and the hemp and so forth. Improved the country no end. Now the Africans say it's all theirs, but what did they ever do to it? Never even laid claim to it. So frankly they should prove it's theirs, or put their money where their mouth is. Stop getting up in arms about it all and show willing.'

Meg made noises now to show she was listening. The lecture was the price of friendship with Mrs Bromley. Although it varied a little from day to day, depending on what pearls of wisdom Mr Bromley brought home with him, basically it always followed the same course. And once she had it off her chest, Mrs Bromley became again the generous, toto-hugging settler's wife most people knew her as. Meg could have told Mrs Bromley that the Africans couldn't buy the land, or lease it, because the British had made sure of it, drawing things up to favour their own, because that was what George had told her. But she didn't, because she didn't share Mrs Bromley's concerns, nor did she want an argument.

Meg didn't lay claim to anything out here, except her children. Even her precious patch of garden was borrowed, and she knew that when she returned home, Africa would take back the ground very quickly. She looked around Mrs

Bromley's drawing room. Old paintings, of ancestors, bowls of fruit and dead birds, hung on the walls. There were delicate tables with wood inlay in chequerboard style that Meg didn't dare put her drink down on. On the floor was a large patterned rug that Mrs Bromley said was from Persia, and the sofas were plumped with green velvet cushions. A glass-fronted cupboard was full of silver objects and figurines – shepherdesses and pierrots. Except for the mosquitoes and the view from the windows, this drawing room might have been in deepest England, and Mrs Bromley, seated in her flowered glory, was queen. But it wasn't Meg's England, and she no more belonged to this room than she did to the Africans' thatched rondavels.

Through the window Meg watched Will running across the lawn. He was chasing after Johnty Bromley, who at seven years old had all the glamour of the older child.

'Are you sending Johnty to England for school?' Meg said.

'In September,' Mrs Bromley said, and Meg saw her shoulders drop as she said it. 'He'll be eight by then. Mr Bromley insists.'

After Will was born Meg had written to her mother: 'His name is William Alan Garrowby. Alan for George's father, and William for my brother. He will be known as Will.'

She wrote, too, that she and the baby were doing well and that she hoped it would not be too long before his grandmother saw him.

She didn't hear back for three months and when a letter did finally arrive, there was no word written about her baby son. No congratulations, no hope of seeing him, no word of support. Nothing.

'Is Johnty looking forward to it?' Meg said.

'He thinks it's all castles and kings and whatnot.'

'My mother thinks Africa is all elephants and Boers.'

Mrs Bromley laughed.

'Anyway, it's got to be done,' she said, 'and if it were done, then best it were done quickly, as the poet said.'

Meg liked Joyce Bromley. She was a salt of the earth kind of woman, like Mrs Gilmer back home. She knew her liking was at least partly expedient. The Bromleys lived just down the hill. When George was away, they were her first port of call in an emergency. Besides which the two men were about to go into business together.

'You didn't think of going back to England with Johnty, then?' she said.

'To live? Goodness, no. The other two have coped. Besides, Mr Bromley needs me here. Expensive business, educating one's children. You'll discover that soon enough.'

'I can't bear the thought.' The words came out before Meg could check them, and behind them the press of tears.

Mrs Bromley tsked again.

'Heavens, girl, Will is only four years old. You've got years yet.'

Meg felt Mrs Bromley study her face.

'You're upset about something,' Mrs Bromley said. 'Distracted.'

'I'm absolutely fine.'

'A disagreement with George?'

Meg shook her head.

'It's just been a bit of a morning.'

So she told her about Henry's fever, which had broken now, thank goodness, and about Will being lost and found again. She didn't mention the letter in her bag, tucked flat between her purse and the shopping list, and Mrs Bromley made sympathetic noises and mixed Meg another gin and orange squash, despite her earlier protestation.

'You'll work it off, digging your lovely garden,' she said, putting it down firmly beside Meg. 'But listen, arguments about the children going away are as old as the hills. We all have them. Wife in tears, husband with his chin out, stubborn. You know that.'

Meg looked at her. That was it, of course. Children going away. A child had gone away from her home and they never talked about it, her mother and her. Never mentioned it. Never said his name. And then she wrote his name in a letter. Dared to. Dared to miss him, to wish for him, and the letter drowned with the ship. So then she placed his name next to her heart and gave it to her son. Her mother couldn't silence it now.

'Let me guess. . .' Mrs Bromley went on. '. . . George has had the boys' names down for prep school since birth, and of course they must go because what was good for him, family tradition, etc etc.'

Meg wondered if it was possible that Mrs Bromley didn't know what kind of background she came from, or George.

'He only told me a month ago,' she said. 'Will's to go to a prep school on the South Downs. He won't even be eight years old when he goes. George mentioned it in the same breath that he told me about the plan for the dairy farm.'

She thought: I couldn't bear to cross a single road or walk along a pavement or past a church. My son will have to cross an ocean.

'Doesn't make one feel better about these things when one's husband compares one's children to prize Friesians,' Mrs Bromley said. 'I've explained that to John I don't know how many times. But he's a shrewd businessman, your husband. Too canny for the colonial service. I'm glad he's going into business with John, because frankly, John is good enough with the livestock, and with the Africans, and he can tell if the coffee's roasted well, if it comes to that; but he hasn't got a business head. Not like George has.'

'George has certainly read enough books,' Meg said.

'Think he's done more than just read the books,' Mrs Bromley said. 'He's done jolly well for himself, and for you and the boys, and well done him, I say.'

'I don't know very much about George's work,' Meg said. 'He won't tell me very much.'

'Well, you're a brave girl,' Mrs Bromley said puzzlingly. And Meg had that old sense of not being told the whole story. George called her his little woman when she asked him something he didn't want to answer and Mrs Bromley told her she was a brave girl. She didn't remember what her mother had said, but then she had given up asking her for answers when she was still small.

They ate their lunch on the veranda, the two women at one table and the little boys at another.

'It's just the cards table. A bit rickety. But frightfully grown up for them,' Mrs Bromley said.

Behind her, Meg heard Johnty whisper something and Will giggle.

'Mind your manners or you can go and eat in the kitchen,' Mrs Bromley said. 'Johnty, you're the big boy, so you can show William what to do.'

After that the boys behaved impeccably, tucking their napkins under their chins and cutting their fish into small pieces. When Mrs Bromley was called away by her houseboy, Meg listened in to their conversation.

'We can play soldiers again after,' Will said. 'Cos I can run faster when I'm not hungry. I can run fast as Njombo nearly.'

'Who's Njombo?'

'I play soldiers with him. He's nearly as big as you.'

'Is he one of the totos that runs after the motor car?' Johnty said.

Will nodded.

'He puts his hand on my window.'

'Then he deserves to be run over. That's what my father says.'

'Well, my daddy thinks he's brave,' Will said.

'Anyway, it's silly, playing with Natives. When I go away to England I'll play rugby. Only baby children play with the Natives.'

Mrs Bromley came back with a shopping list.

'I'm going into Kandula this afternoon. Anything you need?'

Meg shook her head.

'Of course you've been in already today. Lost your boy and found him again.'

'Yes,' Meg said. And she thought: I can't open the letter on my own too. I can't bear to.

Meg had made her garden just out of sight of the house, where the land dipped down to form a small hollow. A cluster of juniper trees and wild fig gave some shade and she'd made flowerbeds and what she thought of as a glade with English flowers: daffodils and jonquils, harebells and tiny violets that flowered suddenly, rapidly, once the long rains came. In one corner there was a small pond and it was dense now with yellow flag irises and water lilies. Sometimes she'd see a frog, submerged to its shoulders, and she'd watch the frog and the frog would watch her back, unblinking, unmoved. In the flowerbeds she had planted roses and lavender, hollyhocks and pansies, not with any great design, but because they were the flowers her mother grew and so they were familiar.

The sun was fierce now. She could feel the press of it through the sleeves of George's old shirt, through the brim of her hat. Later, once the children were in bed for the night and the air was cooler, she would carry down watering cans. She thought perhaps she'd read her mother's letter there then, if the lantern gave enough light. But for now there was weeding

and deadheading to do, and she would cut some fresh flowers. She bent down and pushed her fingers into the earth. It
was so warm and so dry. This piece of garden was hers. It
was her own place where she need not pretend to anything.
Sometimes she would talk to herself amongst these English
flowers. She'd tell herself that she'd been a fool, or that she'd
been wise and all would be fine. Sometimes she was very sad
and she'd find herself crying, the tears lost in the dark soil.

Jim. This was the only place she'd allow herself to think of
him. The only place she'd name him. Jim. Jim. Jim. Again and
again, till the name was no more than a sound. She wondered
if he were alive; she'd looked for his name in the lists, but
she could have missed it. And if he were alive, she wondered
whether he was married now. That gave her a stab, like catching her thumb on a rose thorn. She wondered if he had a child;
if he had another son. Sometimes when Will laughed, she saw
Jim's grin and Will had a way of remarking, already, that was
so like Jim that it shocked her: 'Phew,' he'd exclaim, or 'Wow,'
and it must have been in the gesture he made that she saw Jim
standing there, on her cabin floor, and she would turn away.

What if George suddenly remembered the soldier from
the lifeboat who watched them, who watched her, when
the others had turned away again? What if he remembered
her looking back as they left the quayside, the last of all her
looking, her longing over those endless days on the endless
sea; and the way that the soldier lifted his head to her, eyes
steady, then lowered his glance again?

Meg cut white roses for the bowl in the dining room.

Her fear was absurd. But she still looked at her son and saw another man's child. Will had been born full term, a dark-haired scrappy bit of a baby. This surprised the doctor because long fingernails and flaky skin were a sure sign of an overdue baby, but the parents were quite sure about the conception date, and the baby was healthy and the mother was fine, so he didn't enquire further.

'The spit of you,' he only said to her, and lifted his hat.

Then carefully Meg bit down each of her baby's nails, and gently she rubbed baby lotion into his dry skin. And when George came home later, they looked together at their sleeping baby, and George laid his hand on his forehead like a blessing.

Once she had filled the basket with roses, Meg walked back up to the house. Henry still slept and she was loath to wake him after his fever, though she hoped this didn't mean he would be awake during the night. In the kitchen the air smelt sweet with Victoria sponge. Will knelt on a chair at the table and stirred a bowl of butter icing with a wooden spoon. Elbow hooked out, head down so he could bring all his small boy strength to bear, he looked like he was stirring with his life.

Standing behind him, Meg made a circle in his fair hair with her finger.

'Crown fit for a king,' she said.

Will kept on, intent with his task.

'Kibaki found a snake inside the house,' he said after a moment.

'Did he?' Meg said. 'What kind?'

His hair turned clockwise at the crown, twisting like a whirlpool. She followed the thread round with a finger.

'A python,' Will said. 'A young one, only as long as I am.'

He shook his head with an irritated shrug as if an insect were annoying him.

She thought: he's the age I was then.

'And we gave him some milk,' he said.

'You gave him some milk,' she said, and she thought: he's still nearly a baby. I was nearly a baby still.

'Don't you want to know the story why?' Will said. Ducking away from her hand, he turned around and looked up at her. 'Kibaki told me.'

'Yes, I do,' she said.

She sat at the table and took the wooden spoon from him and dipped it into the butter icing.

'Perfect,' she said.

'It's because if a python comes into your house, then it's a spirit really. So you have to look after it.'

'A spirit?' Meg said.

She wondered where Kibaki was, and she decided she would wake Henry up in half an hour's time.

'Kibaki said it's your ancestor's spirit and you have to be nice to it.'

'You have to be nice to it?' If she woke him soon, he'd probably sleep tonight, she thought. He was a good sleeper generally.

Will nodded his head. 'Yes, so it will talk to God and keep you safe from bad things.'

Meg looked round at Will. 'Was there really a python in the

house?' she said.

Will nodded his head vigorously. 'I told you that already. Ask Kibaki,' he said.

'And where is it now?'

Will waved his hand, a miniature parody of adult nonchalance. 'It's gone out, of course, because it finished up the milk, so you won't be able to see it.' He stood up. 'We can put the icing on the cake for Daddy tomorrow.'

Now Meg was frightened. She shouted for Kibaki, for Sita. Telling Will to stay where he was, she took a broom and ran to the children's bedroom. Henry slept peacefully. Carefully she checked beneath the cot, beneath the bed, behind the curtains, ruffling the mosquito nets to be absolutely sure. No snake; nothing lurked, and she closed the door securely behind her. Her snake was not sacred. It was a malevolent creature that could make its way silently into her house and threaten her family.

'Kibaki!' she shouted again. She would not have him feeding milk to a snake in her house, and she would not have him teaching Kikuyu stories to her son. She had her own stories. A python could swallow a goat or a pig, or a deer or a child. Mrs Pritchard knew someone whose little girl was snatched.

'Sita!' she shouted.

Where were they? There was too much danger in this country, too much to be frightened of, and she could feel the panic rise in her, and she knew she must sit down. Pulling out a chair, she sat at the dining room table, laying her arms flat on the dark varnished wood. It felt cool and un-urgent.

'Come on,' she said. 'Breathe. Nice and deep.'

And as her racing heart slowed, she made herself take stock. She had two healthy children and a good husband. A house and garden she could never have dreamed of. Henry's fever had broken and Will was not lost. There was the letter, but how bad could the news be? She had made her life here now; it would be sad if someone had died, but not so sad: Mrs Gilmore, or Reverend Rogers. Probably it was a piece of news like that. Probably it was, and she pushed the thought of it away from her because whatever it was, she would wait till George was home. And Yusuf could bring the tea out to the veranda and she could praise Will for making such a beautiful cake. She opened the French windows. She'd call him now, and have Sita wake up Henry.

Walking along the veranda was like being on a ship's deck and she stopped in her tracks. She almost thought she could hear Mrs Richardson's voice, its higher pitch than hers. 'Come and join me,' she'd be saying. 'Come here.' But Meg didn't want to think about the ship, or Mrs Richardson, not when she was on her own; never on her own. She looked out over the plain with all its browns and reds, to the far hills. They looked softer in the afternoon light, more inviting, as if you could take a gentle walk in them, like walking through the English countryside. Perhaps they could go on a safari, her and George. It was what people did. They said they saw sights they'd never forget. Never want to forget. And George could tell her all about things. He'd like that. He knew so much about the country now. She thought: he'd have known what to do about the python.

Perhaps it was Will's voice that had brought Mrs Richardson to mind; because as she walked round the house, she could hear him clearly, speaking nineteen to the dozen, his voice high and excited. Then she heard Sita, and Yusuf, and finally a fourth voice, a man's, and this voice was familiar and unexpected. Quickening her step, Meg came round the side of the house, and there he was. He was home a day early, and just hearing him she could steady herself and feel things become plainer and more solid again. The letter from home became simply a letter from home.

He had his back to her and was giving an instruction to Yusuf, while beside him Will hopped from foot to foot with excitement.

'George!' she said.

Yusuf gave a short bow and hurried off and George turned.

'You're home early,' she said, and he smiled.

She felt his glance take in her face and her clothes and she was glad that she'd changed out of his old shirt and put up her hair again. These things mattered to him.

His clothes were coloured pink with red dust and his skin was grimy, the pale hair on his arms and legs and at his neck matted into webs. His eyes were red-rimmed, though whether from the dust or lack of sleep, she didn't yet know. Bending towards her, he kissed her on the cheek and she smelt sweat and an oily, rancid smell she knew from the town, and which he always had when he came home from these trips.

'What's for tea then?' he said, which was his way of saying how glad he was to be home.

'Will?' she said. 'Tell your father what is for tea. Lucky it was done a day early.'

'I made a cake, Daddy,' Will said.

'What, all by yourself?'

'With Kibaki's help,' Meg said, reminded already of how exacting, how ungenerous George could be with Will.

'And where's the little fellow?' George said.

'He's sleeping,' Meg said.

'He's usually awake at this time.'

Will tapped at his father's elbow.

'So you can have some, because you're back beforehand,' he said.

George looked down at Will as if only just noticing him.

'One says early, not beforehand,' George said. 'I'll go and wash up before tea.'

And he picked up his valise and went inside.

Meg could feel Will's disappointment.

'Did you see how dusty your father was?' she said. 'He'll feel better when he's changed into fresh clothes and had a wash.'

Meg busied herself and ten minutes later the tea was laid on the veranda and Henry sat on Sita's lap, dopey-eyed but properly dressed, drinking a bottle of milk. Will's hair had been combed and Meg had tidied herself. When George came out in fresh-pressed shirt and shorts, his shoes polished to a high shine, she nudged Will and he approached his father with his hand out.

'Welcome back, Father,' he said. 'We are very pleased to see you.'

George gave a short smile and he took Will's hand.

'I hope you've been a good boy,' he said. 'Obedient to your mother.'

There was a pause, like a breath held, and then Will nodded vigorously. George studied him.

'Shall we ask her?' he said, and he turned Will round to face her, manoeuvring the little boy by his shoulders like a wind-up toy.

Meg looked at her son. There was panic in his face and his blue eyes looked wide, unseeing.

'Go on,' George said, giving Will a tap. 'Ask her: "Have I been a good boy?" I'll expect her to give a truthful reply.'

'Have I been a good boy?' Will's voice was a monotone, and he looked straight ahead so that he seemed to be directing his question at Meg's waistband. She saw him bite his lip and shut his eyes. She looked over at George, waiting for her to answer.

'Yes,' she said. 'You have, actually. You've been a fine little man, while your father has been away.'

'Good,' George said, sitting down, matter-of-fact, inquisition over. 'Glad to hear it. So now let's have some tea. And what about the little fellow?'

George was full of questions about his younger son. How had he been eating? Any teeth coming through? Was she sure this fever was just a passing malady? Let him have a hold; Sita would trust him not to drop his own son? This last a joke he made each time he took the baby. And maybe it was simply because Henry was still so small; or it was because George had been away for a while, but Meg didn't think so. Because he had never held Will in this way, or gazed at him like this. He had always been correct with Will, but with Henry he was tender.

Perhaps when Henry too became a little boy, then George would become firm and distant with him. It might be something he thought it necessary for a boy to learn from his father, if he was to advance in the world. Or perhaps, she thought, she just didn't know how fathers should be. Her father had disappeared so early that she had only a few memories of him: shaving in the morning; standing at the stove with hot bricks; and sometimes it was just a smell, like a flick in the air, on a busy street and she didn't know what it was she remembered, but always then she thought of him: a big, dark-haired figure who stood strong as a rock in front of her, and was gone.

Husband and wife sat on as the sun dropped low.

'See how close the hills appear?' George said. 'As if you could just step into them, like stepping into the next room. The rains must be very close, thank God.'

'The wind is up, too,' she said. 'Always a sign.'

Yusuf had cleared the tea things and Will had been released from the table. Sita was seeing to his boiled egg supper in the kitchen and preparing some ground rice for the baby.

The cicadas struck up and the first bats came out to dance.

'How was the trip?' Meg said.

'Fine. All fine.'

George didn't like being pressed about his work, but she felt it was polite to ask.

'You?' he said. 'Any news?'

'Not really,' she said. 'A letter from my mother last week with the usual. And Kibaki's daughter continues to be ill, and Yusuf said his brother is doing well in his cattle trading. I had lunch with Joyce Bromley today and she said that John is looking forward to your business venture.'

'Good,' he said. 'I'm going to nip down now and have a quick word with him. There's time, before dinner?'

Meg nodded, and said no more about her day. She didn't mention that Kibaki had fed a python with milk in the house that afternoon, nor did she mention Will's disappearance, or his game in the trees with the totos; nor did she mention the second letter from her mother, still unopened in her bag.

Dear Meg,

It is the evening at last and soon I will go to bed. Dr Fanshaw has given me some pills but I don't think I will sleep. I am sorry for this news and it is difficult to write down, but until I have done so and put the letter in the post, I will have no chance of rest.

Yesterday I was visited by a policeman. Not Sergeant Millar, who you may remember, but another from the town. He held his helmet in his hands so I knew he came with news.

A body was found in the woods near Merestead. They were dragging the lake to make it deeper for fishing, and they brought up the skeleton of a boy. I don't know how they knew it might be Will after all this time, but they did. It was the right size for him. There was a St Christopher medal around its neck. I knew it was him when I saw the medal. I put it there the morning he went.

They have dragged the lake in case of another, but there isn't one. God only knows about your father.

Everybody has been very kind. Mrs Rogers has sat in with me. She says she will help with the funeral. It will be next week after they have finished with him.

It is terrible to know this for sure though I have feared it for many years. But it is a comfort to be here, so close, and to have the support around me of people who knew him too. I am sorry you are so very far away and that you cannot bury him with me. I will be glad to have him laid in the earth to rest at last.

It will perhaps be even harder for you in that strange country amongst people who never knew him. Your own sons must be your comfort, and George, of course.

Soon I will go to the place, to see where my boy has been all these years. Perhaps you will think this funny, but I've been expecting that knock on the door for so long and now it has come I feel relieved.

Meg folded the letter up.

'Breathe,' she said. 'Nice and deep.'

In a few minutes, when she could, she would stand up. Then she would leave the bag and the letter in her bedroom, shut the door firmly and go to the kitchen. With George home, she'd make an omelette for supper, in place of the boiled egg.

George would drink a beer. Afterwards, she expected, he would read one of his farming books and smoke a pipe and she would go and water her garden.

He'd been lying there all those years in the cold and the dark. While she'd been growing bigger, growing up, he'd been getting smaller and smaller, shrinking to nothing more than bones, a small boy's bones, and the St Christopher medal around his neck to bring him safe home. The day had stopped dead for him, and for her it had never ended.

And what about her father? Strong as a rock, she remembered him. There, then gone. What had happened to him that day?

She felt a pause in her body; or was it in the room? Then rage. It didn't come from nowhere; it wasn't new, but she'd never turned towards it before. It was like facing into a wind so strong that it forces the breath from your mouth and the tears from your eyes.

'You bastard,' she said slowly, quietly. 'You bastard with no bones. You're not there, in that lake. You didn't die and you didn't come back. You never even came back to tell us.'

Her voice was hard and low.

'You left him and his body, and you left us.'

'Mummy?'

She started. It was Will's voice, sleepy and uncertain. 'Mummy?'

And when she turned, there he was on the threshold, more asleep than awake, a little, sleepy boy she would go to and reassure and tuck back in to his bed.

'What are you doing?' she said gently, and she felt her rage drop and relief touch her forehead like a calm hand. She picked him up. He was warm and soft-skinned. 'Did you have a dream?'

He nodded.

'Is Daddy here?'

She stroked his hair.

'You'll see him in the morning,' she said, kissing his cheek. 'Sweet dreams.'

In the kitchen Meg broke eggs and whipped them. She boiled potatoes and cabbage. She opened a tin of ham. The night sky was full of stars, same as every night. When she was a child somebody had told her that each star was the soul of someone who had died; she didn't understand then why that was meant to be comforting, and she didn't understand now. Insects crashed against the kitchen window, trying for the light.

The omelette was yellow like the sun. She cut it in two, a smaller half and a larger, and took the food into the dining room. George was back and waiting. She smiled.

'It's a proper dinner tomorrow,' she said. 'Yusuf bought a piece of beef.'

George nodded. He studied his food, then lifted his knife and fork.

She watched him eat. He was methodical with this, as with all things, and he ate steadily, keeping his eyes on the plate. She had learned it was better not to distract him during this, and she waited until he had nearly finished.

'George,' she said.

He looked at her plate. Her food was untouched.

'Not hungry?'

She shook her head.

'Mind if I . . .?' he said, pointing.

She shook her head again and pushed her plate towards him.

'Not coming down with something?' he said, his mouth full with cabbage and ham and egg.

'No,' she said, and she thought her voice was steady, but something made him pause and look up.

She shut her eyes and watched the flecks and fragments that gathered behind her sight in all their shades of darkness.

'What's the matter?'

George's voice was solid; she could hear his concern, and she could hear the flick of anxiety behind it.

'What's happened?' he said.

'There was another letter from my mother. I waited till you came back to open it.'

He read the letter in the same way that he ate his dinner, then folded it up and pushed it back across the shiny table.

'I've known, really,' Meg said. 'For years. Else he'd have come to find us.'

'Your brother, you mean?'

'Yes.'

George stood up.

'You'd better eat something,' he said, and he left the room.

She looked across to the windows, to the view across the hills, but the night had come down fully and all she could see in the black glass was the table and the chair backs and herself.

George returned with a plate of buttered bread and honey. He pulled his chair beside her and put his arm around her shoulders.

'At least it's settled,' he said.

She noticed that the bread was cut straight and the butter spread evenly and that the honey made a smooth patina of yellow in the middle. He never cooked, never made his own breakfast even. She took a bite and the sweetness made her gulp.

'You'll have a place to go to now,' he said. 'To remember him, that is.'

She thought: I've never forgotten him, not even for a moment. Only now he'll only be there, and I'll never hope to find him anywhere else.

They sat together in the darkened room and she finished the bread and honey.

'You should sit on the veranda and smoke your pipe,' she said. 'Please. I'd like you to do that. And I'll water the garden.'

She carried a watering can in one hand and a lantern in the other. Bushes and plants loomed in and out of the dark. The rains would be here soon, but she would water her garden tonight.

She'd leave Africa, she knew now. When Will went away to school, she'd return to England. She didn't want to live with so much water between them. Or perhaps she'd leave before then and make her own home, not a borrowed one, and her own garden.

At the pond she stopped and listened. The air was full of foreign sounds and the wind was whipping up. Her eyes swam. Clouds had covered the sky and the night had grown darker. She set the lantern down by the pond so that it threw a shadow of light over the water, and she wrapped her arms around herself.

'Will,' she cried, but softly because this Will, this brother of hers, he was lost and gone, and it was no good searching for him any longer.

She heard the rain even before she felt it – a rush of sound, a sigh – then it was falling, quietly, surely. She knelt down and the rich, warm smells of the wet earth, from which all things came and to which all returned, rose around her.

FIRE

The light came across the bed so bright, it was like a blow to the head. He woke with a start and lay there dazed. Then smiled. It was going to be the best day.

There was no hurry to be up. The dawn had barely broken, the birds still busy with their shouting, but he was awake. He watched the baubles of light run across the ceiling, then turned and watched Benjamin. He would sleep for hours yet, or till he was woken.

Stretching the night from his arms, Will swung out of the bedclothes and pulled a sweater over his pyjamas. On the landing he stopped and listened. The house was quiet. His father gone to work already, thank God; his brother and sister still sleeping. He took the stairs to the half landing in one and locked the bathroom door behind him. The first piss of the day. Aiming for the deepest point in the bowl, he let go and listened. He liked it that the sound of his piss had got deeper with his voice. He'd stood here like this since he was small enough that his mother had put out a box for him to stand on. This bathroom that he knew so well: the creak of the seat when he pushed it up, and the brown linoleum, and the line of shells on the windowsill. Better than standing on cold tiles in the middle of a row of bleary boys and pissing into a trough with no time and no privacy to enjoy it.

He pulled the chain and set the seat down again. Other

boys in other families left it up – he'd noticed when he stayed at their houses – but his mother was insistent on this, as she was about few other things where he was concerned, and he obeyed her. On his way downstairs Will mapped out the day, his sleeping friend tucked into a corner of his mind like a gift.

In the kitchen the wireless talked about the weather. Will put the kettle on the stove to boil. He ducked through the back door and found his mother in the greenhouse. She was in her dressing gown, the sleeves rolled up out of the way, tending her plants. He noticed the fine hair at the nape of her neck, lit up by the sun, and wondered fleetingly whether his father ever stroked it.

Without turning from what she was doing, Meg beckoned to him.

'They don't like our soil,' she said, pointing to some green shoots in a pot. 'But sometimes I can fool them for a while and convince them that they do.'

'Would you like a cup of tea?' he said, and she looked up surprised, then smiled at her tall son and pulled his head down to kiss him on the forehead.

He made the tea carefully, using her favourite teapot and the blue china with flowers round the edge that she liked best.

'You're up very early. Benjamin still asleep?' she said.

He nodded.

'Sensible boy,' she said. 'And you didn't wake the little ones.'

'I was a mouse,' he said. 'Everything's still quiet.'

He sat down in the old wicker chair and watched his

mother. She worked on with her plants and every so often she would stop and sip her tea, carefully so as not to make a noise, and place the cup down gently, making only the softest clink on the saucer.

It was nearly perfect, sitting here like this and Benjamin asleep upstairs, and the day still so early it was all ahead of them.

'I'm taking Benjamin to Shining Sands today,' he said.

'You've checked the tides? You've listened to the forecast?' Meg said.

'It's going to be beautiful. We'll try for some mackerel on the way, cook them on driftwood.'

'Bring some home, if you catch enough,' Meg said.

He could feel an erection rising with the thought of the day and he pulled his knees up onto the seat, circling them with his arms, but still he was glad his mother had her back to him.

'He's never done that kind of thing before,' he said.

'Poor city boy,' she said and he grinned because she knew that Benjamin was anything but poor, and because she spoke of him with such affection.

'You'll take out the Wayfarer?'

He nodded.

'Better today than tomorrow for the trip,' Meg said, 'what with the dance.'

Will's stomach flipped. Somewhere in the house a clock struck the hour.

'The dance?' he said.

'The Lavery girl. I told you about it when you came home.

It's her eighteenth tomorrow; a big bash. They're delighted Benjamin can come too; they're a bit short on boys.'

'I forgot,' he said. 'I haven't told Benjamin.'

'I'm sure he won't mind. He's a well brought up boy. He'll charm them all.'

'He doesn't charm Father,' Will said. 'And I don't even know Barbara Lavery. I used to play with her when I was eight years old.' His erection faltered. 'I don't want to go, and I don't want to take Benjamin. He won't know anybody.'

Surely she wouldn't make him. He didn't have anything to say to girls and he hated dances. Hated all the guff and pretence.

Meg tamped another seedling safe in its pot and eased the next free from the gather of roots.

'You're going, William, with or without Benjamin,' she said.

He went into the garden. His feet still had their night softness and the path grit was needle-sharp. Jaw clenched, he reached the lawn. His father's lawn, a stretch of sheer green, where not a daisy, not a spindle of moss, not a single lucky clover leaf could find a place.

'It's because of Africa,' his mother had told him. 'You can't imagine, you were small. He used to dream of green.'

'Petit bourgeois,' Will thought, but he kept it to himself.

This early morning the grass was silver with dew and his feet left trails. So soft, so cool it was underfoot that a thread of sensation ran through him, and he ran round the house and stood beneath his open window.

'Ben,' he called up. Benjamin should see him running here, should join him even. But even as he called, he hoped his friend still slept because his anger with his mother had slipped away into the grass. Tomorrow was tomorrow – he would find a way with the dance – and today they were sailing to Shining Sands, just him and Benjamin, and it would be glorious. He ran back round the house; he would sit in the wicker chair while the day came in, and tell his mother his ambitions. She always loved to hear him talk like that if they were alone.

A clock struck the quarter hour, ringing out its thwarted quarter phrase. He didn't even know that he'd heard it but it checked him and he heard his father's voice in his head: 'I don't want to hear what you might want to do. I want to hear what you will do, and when and how.'

He had been frightened of his father when he was small, eager to please, but bewildered as to what was wanted. Now he was contemptuous. The man was so cluttered about by his own rules and measurements that he never had time to live. At work by six every morning, home by six each evening. A measure of sherry and the winding and adjustment of the clocks, glass in hand, by six fifteen. Then the children. Six clocks, and three children. The clocks he gave two and a half minutes each, and the children: they must each account for themselves in ten. That left fifteen minutes for the *Telegraph* crossword before Meg rang the dinner bell at seven.

'Calibration and estimation,' George would say. 'The successful man makes it his business to know his subject before tackling it,' he would say. 'Know thine enemies, young man.'

And Will would nod politely and think: You are my enemy.

A second clock chimed, breaking Will's dark reverie and he headed for the kitchen. He could smell bacon and he remembered that he was hungry.

Meg stood at the stove.

'Ready in five minutes,' she said. 'Benjamin's can go into the warming oven.'

'I'll have to wake him,' he said, 'or he'll sleep till noon. And we have to catch the tide right.'

She turned round and ruffled his hair. She had to reach up, now he was taller than she was.

'You've inherited the early mornings from your father,' she said.

Will scowled and shrugged away. He hated comparisons with his father.

'I'm not like him,' he said.

'I was only speaking about the early mornings,' his mother said mildly.

'He thinks everyone should be up early. He thinks everyone should work at things all the time and do the same as him. As if he has a monopoly on what is right,' he said. He had never spoken of his father like this before, not to anyone, not to his mother, but his chest was tight with an anger that had flared on the instant. 'I think he's wrong; very wrong. I don't think everybody should do the same as anybody else,' he said.

'You haven't lived his life, William.'

'No I haven't, because I'm not him. But try telling him that.'

'He's worked as hard as a man can work. The years in Africa on his own, working himself to the bone, all of us safely in England, so he could make this home for his family . . .'

'As he never stops telling us. I know.'

'And we've sent you to an excellent school . . .'

'Please, Mother.'

'So that you can have the education that he didn't get, that I certainly didn't get; that teaches you to think for yourself; dare I say it, to be rude, even, as you are being now . . .'

Will couldn't stop himself and he slammed his hand down on the table.

'I've heard you and Father arguing about that education. You didn't want me to go away to school, you don't want Henry to go in September, and you certainly don't want Emma to go. But he played that card, I heard him: "If they don't go to the school I choose, then I'm not paying for them to go any-where." That's not a shared decision, that's his tyranny. You thought you had to give in, to give us what you didn't get, a better start in the world and all of that. But it's all on his terms. This house, this life, us, we all have to do it, all of it, on his terms.'

'You eavesdropped.' Meg spoke quietly.

'Yes, but what he said . . .'

'It was a private conversation.'

'But what he said . . .'

'Stop now,' she said, and he stopped.

Her voice was level, but she was so angry he thought she might hit him. He pictured her battering at his chest, the pair of them like a piece of corny melodrama, one of those black and white pictures from before the war.

'Sit,' she said.

He slid round the table and sat slouched down on the bench, his back against the wall, his arms on the scrubbed surface. It was his old place though he had grown so much these last six months that there was barely room.

She took the frying pan off the heat and sat down opposite. She was white-lipped.

'When you leave home, then you will choose how you live your life . . .' she said and she paused.

He sat in his pyjamas and sweater facing his mother over the table, so near to her that he could see a money spider scrambling in her hair. She was as angry as he'd ever seen her. She reached and put her hand on his chin like a command, lifting his head so that he met her gaze; and the kitchen, his father, Benjamin asleep, his siblings: all were vaporised and there was only the two of them in the whole universe.

When she spoke again, she did so slowly, as if each word had been chosen with great deliberation.

'. . .You will choose how you live your life. And as you are my son, William – as my son – I tell you that you, and you alone, must do the choosing.'

Her words were fierce and opaque. They were older than her anger and fiercer than a wish. They rang through his head and he thought: this is like a play; we are acting something. But it was also real, and he knew he must remember what she'd said.

Then Meg took her hand from his chin and stood up.

'I don't ever want to hear you talk about your father like that again. If you have something to say, say it to his face or not at all. You'll be a man soon and you must start to behave like one.'

Will sat in silence as his mother went on with her cooking. She had told him something he understood clearly and something that he understood not at all. He looked across at the farther wall to the picture of the knots. He knew each by heart: the clove hitch, the bowline, the reef knot. He had eaten every childhood meal at this table and in this place, and he had learned the knots without knowing it. Now, as his eyes ran across them, he could feel the rope in his fingers: the rough intransigence of wet hemp, the clean moves of the knot, the tug to bring it to bear, that sure satisfaction of a knot well made.

'Your breakfast is ready. And you'd better wake that sleeping beauty friend of yours before too long, else his will be shrivelled and dry and the tide will have gone.'

Will started. His mother's voice had a mock-jovial edge and he was grateful to her.

'I'll eat mine first, then wake him,' he said, because he wasn't ready yet to share the room with anybody else. Just for a few more minutes he wanted to keep his mother to himself.

Benjamin slept like a dancer. That's what he reminded Will of. Lying on his side with one arm above his head and the other out across the floor, his fingers spread like an invitation; and his legs leaping as if caught by some ancient sculptor on an ancient frieze.

'Greek boy,' Will whispered, 'wake up.'

He bent towards him, desire rising, and another morning he might have wedged his bedroom door shut, then put his fingers through Benjamin's hair and run them down to the crook of his dancing hip. But today they were sailing to Shining Sands and he checked himself. There was no time to be lost. And besides this, there was something too much for Will about leaving his mother downstairs and turning so soon to Ben.

So he put his hand on the sleeping boy's shoulder and shook him. Gently at first, then harder, but Benjamin slept on. Only groaned a little and turned away, his breath still a sleeper's breathing, deep and even.

'Wake up, Ben.'

A note of impatience crept into Will's voice.

'Come on. Time for breakfast, Benjamin Mayer.'

The minutes were ticking by and the tide waited for no man, most especially not for an idle boy. He winced with the thought because it was his father's. His father, who disliked boats of every kind and was never a slave to the tide and yet who chose to live so near to the sea that he could taste the salt on his tongue. Will shook his friend again, gripping his shoulders more fiercely, digging his fingers down into the soft muscle.

'It's a perfect day. Come on. Get up, or I'll get mother's bell and ring it in your ear.'

Still Benjamin lay sleeping and Will stood up, frustrated,

his thoughts slipping into violence. He would go to the bathroom for cold water; he would beat him with something, a
hairbrush like the matron used, the belt on the back of the
chair.

Then hands grabbed at him, his legs buckled and he fell,
tumbled to the covers, Benjamin on top of him, his face close,
laughing.

'Come on, fight me,' Benjamin said. 'Perhaps you'll win
today,' teasing him, because both knew that Benjamin was the
stronger.

'Ben, don't,' Will said, and 'Don't . . .' again, as Benjamin
pinioned his arms and leaned close.

'You woke me in that brutal way and you won't even kiss
me?' Benjamin said, keeping his voice low because Henry and
Emma slept in the next room.

'Mother has your breakfast waiting, and the day's so clear
you can see the colour of Brigstone Rock and I'm taking you
to Shining Sands, and the tide . . .'

Will's voice implored.

'All right.' Benjamin let go Will's arms and stood, and the
two boys dressed in silence. As they were leaving the room,
Will crowned his friend with his sailing cap and kissed him
once on the mouth.

'That's a promise,' he said.

'Have you told your friend about the dance tomorrow?' Meg
said.

A clock struck another quarter and Will wished she had not

brought it up just now.

'I'll tell him as we walk down to the slip,' he said.

'A dance,' Benjamin said, in his bright, talking-to-mothers voice. 'I like dances.' Will looked at him sharply because that wasn't what he'd ever said before, and Benjamin returned a guileless smile.

'You see?' Meg said. 'Not everyone is as dog in the manger as you.'

'It's a girl I've barely met,' Will said. 'Her birthday. I'd forgotten. She wouldn't even notice if I wasn't there. And we won't know anybody.'

'Will seems to think there's no need, ever, to meet any girls,' Meg said.

'There's Emma,' Will said. 'I get on with her perfectly well.'

'And she's nearly seven years old, and your sister.'

Benjamin put down his knife and fork.

'Delicious, Mrs Garrowby. I feel ready for anything. Sailing, dances, you name it.'

'I've said to him: no girls at school, there'll be no girls at Oxford to speak of, and by then you'll be twenty-one years old and any girl, she'll expect you to have some idea of what to do. How to talk to her.'

'You're not finishing those bits?' Will said, pulling Benjamin's plate towards him, and he ate the fried bread and sausage that remained.

'We must go to the dance. You might meet your future wife there,' Benjamin said, poker-faced, and to Meg: 'What kind of dress code is it?'

His mother and Benjamin had charmed each other from the first, and mostly Will enjoyed it. There was something ancient and courtly about their compliments and he was happy to sit and watch. He was mostly happy, too, when they joked at his expense, but this talk about the dance was too raw. He didn't want to meet a girl, or anyone, and it hurt when Benjamin said he should.

'It's casual,' Meg said. 'You'll be fine.'

Will swallowed a last piece of sausage.

'I don't know where you get that appetite, or where you put it. You eat more than Benjamin and he's bigger, taller than you,' she said.

'Will's not as slight as you think, Mrs Garrowby,' Benjamin said. 'I've been up against him. He felt pretty solid then.'

Will looked round at his friend.

'Up against him?' Meg said. She sounded unsure as to what he meant.

Will stood abruptly, and took the plates to the sink.

'In rugby,' Benjamin said.

Rattling the plates Will turned on the tap. He smothered a giggle.

'Ah,' she said.

'Yes, he can see off a fullback with as much force as the next boy.'

'We're going,' Will said. 'Now.'

Meg counted off the items gathered on the table, packing them into a rucksack.

'Sandwiches, beer, griddle, water thermos, oilskins, sweaters,' she said. 'And matches, of course.'

'I've got a lighter,' Will said, fingering the one in his pocket. It was a gift from Benjamin because Will had admired it, though he didn't smoke. 'Surely not oilskins?' His mother was such a pessimist. 'Look at the weather. I tapped the barometer: set fine.'

'It's the sea. You never know,' Meg said. 'The finest sailors have been surprised by the weather. And make sure you wear life jackets.'

'Mother, please,' Will said, because she was treating him like a child, and because he knew what she would say next.

'I watched people die for lack of them,' Meg said.

There was a pause like a heartbeat, then Benjamin spoke. 'I promise we'll wear them,' he said and Will watched his mother's expression ease, and wondered why he hadn't said that first.

'Back and scrubbed up in time for dinner,' Meg said.

'Will you tell Benjamin the story then?' Will said, because she was so serious about the life jackets, and he wanted Ben to know why.

'If you bring me something back from your adventure,' she said.

The lane was still deep in shade as the boys walked down to the water, and the sky overhead was the strongest blue. Will pranced and skipped. He picked a stem from the hedgerow and presented it, mock-gallant, with a bow, to Benjamin.

'For you, Lady's Bedstraw,' he said. 'Should be Lad's Love,

but it doesn't grow wild. Anyway, this is prettier.'

His friend took it laughing and sniffed the froth of yellow flowers.

'Smells of honey,' he said, 'which is not what I've heard from the boys who brag.'

'Don't be vulgar,' Will said. He punched Benjamin's arm. 'We're off. Gone and free.'

'And sleepy,' Benjamin said.

'You'll love it, where I'm taking you.'

'Better be good. What time is it, for God's sake?'

'You can sleep, if you want to, when we get there.'

'I want to sleep now.'

'Did you know that a boy is always taller than his mother? Fact.'

'Will, be quiet.'

The one's grumbling and the other's bounce had the air of something long-practised between them, and in this way they walked the mile from house to water. They passed only the milk lorry and, down near the water, an old man with his rheumy dog.

'William Garrowby, you must be,' the old man said.

'Yes sir,' Will said.

'Look the spit of your mother. Off sailing?'

'Yes sir.'

'Well, watch for the fret later if you're going off far. She's sitting out there, but she'll be coming in this afternoon. Won't be able to see your hand in front of your face.'

'Yes sir.'

The Garrowbys kept their boats a mile out of the village on a small piece of land set a hundred yards or so back from the estuary, next to the Estuary Hotel gardens. The hotel had kept the waterfront for itself, and the Garrowbys ran their boats along a track beside the gardens, which ended in a narrow slipway down to the water. It was characteristic of George that he had thought about what he thought he needed but not about what his children would be capable of. Someone with a different bent of mind or some experience in sailing would have found a piece of land closer to the water from which it was easier to launch boats. But it didn't occur to him to think in this way, and besides, he had got the land for a good price.

At the time George had thought he would take up sailing. He liked what he considered to be sailing's science – the calculations one could apply to wind and water, the charts and so forth – but when it came to the fact, he didn't enjoy it at all. He didn't enjoy how the weather confounded him and he didn't like getting wet, or muddy, or getting it wrong. He didn't like being unreliable. So he stopped sailing almost as soon as he had started, though Will was glad his father had insisted, even so, that his children learned it all thoroughly.

The piece of land comprised a square of grass, two dinghies and a rowing boat, each on its own trolley, and a small shed for gear: oars, life jackets, groundsheet, rugs, outboards, cans of oil, paint, etc. The shed had electric light, routed from the power line high above, and when he was younger, Will had fantasised about living in here. Somehow the electric light made it seem more possible. Looking back, he saw it as his Huck Finn phase and already he felt a rueful affection for that younger boy.

'Perfect time,' he said. 'Twenty minutes and the tide'll be just right to launch straight off the slip. Won't even have to get our plimsolls wet.'

He set about rigging the boat, shouting an occasional instruction to Benjamin. He stowed the rucksacks and the groundsheet in the bow.

'What did the old man mean, about fret? Is it dangerous?' Benjamin said.

'Sea fret. Like mist. It can come in suddenly, but it looks set fair today. Besides, we're not going far out; we could hug the shore, more or less, if we needed to.'

He fetched the oars, life jackets, mackerel lines and bucket. Handing Benjamin a jacket, he pulled his on and tied the bows securely.

'Most important thing is to do what I tell you, when I tell you. Don't want you knocked out by the boom because you didn't go about when I said to.'

'You told me that last time,' Benjamin said.

'Well, I'm telling you again. Anyway, last time we stayed in the estuary. This time we're heading out to open water. Would make rescuing you harder.'

'What's the other thing, then? The slightly less important thing.'

'Watch the wind. That's how you know what to do with the sails. But it often changes, plays tricks on you, so you have to keep watching it. That's what the telltales are for.'

'Telltales?'

'The bits of fabric tied on to the mast. When we're going bang on, when it's singing, they'll all be streaming out behind us – aft that is.'

'And when we get to the beach, then do you stop being so serious?'

Will grinned.

'You just wait,' he said. 'Ready?'

The wind was gusty and unreliable at first and Will had to work the boat hard, beating a slow course upwind towards the mouth of the estuary. There were few other boats moving at this early hour. A bass boat piled high with crab pots chugged its way towards the sea and a boy put a dinghy through its paces, tacking tight, to and fro, between the moored yachts. In another hour the yacht club holiday schedule would be underway and the estuary would be tight with little boats, but for now the two boys had it nearly to themselves.

'You're doing fine,' Will called to Benjamin. 'Watch the boom when we go round. Don't know what the wind will do then.'

But when they came round the point, and out into the open water, the wind steadied into that best of all sailor's winds in those parts, a benign south-westerly, and setting the sails to a broad reach, Will gave himself up to it. He loved this. He loved the speed across the water, driving the tears from his eyes and he loved the fine-tune reading of wind and waves, always trying for the perfect reach. He knew this boat like the back of his hand and his body was sure and strong now, bracing and balancing, finding the equlibirium, the perfect balance. He could sail like this all day and be happy.

'Lean back a bit further,' he called down to Benjamin. 'Trust yourself,' and Benjamin, pulling the sailing cap firmly down on his head, holding fast to the jib sheet line, and with his feet securely hooked, leaned his body back and out over the rushing water.

'If my mother could see me . . .' Benjamin yelled and they laughed, the two boys, with the sheer pleasure of it.

Will had planned to drop the mackerel lines when they were close enough to Brigstone Rock to see the hermit's hut. He'd always done well for mackerel there and Benjamin would like the story of the hermit. He'd let the sails go and they would row for a stretch and see what they could pull in. They were half way there when Benjamin's shout changed the plan.

'Look! Look at the birds!'

Will turned. A crowd of seabirds rushed the churning water, dropping and diving any which way, the seagulls an ungainly mass of wing and beak, the terns impeccable, and a patch of the sea gone to a darker, fretty blue.

'Mackerel!' Will shouted back. 'I'm stopping here.'

Heading the boat into the wind, he let out the sails and they luffed, as ragged and ungainly as the dropping gulls.

'You row and I'll set the lines,' he said.

But there was barely any need to row because the shoal came to them and within minutes, as fast as they could pull in the lines and unhook them the bottom of the boat was covered with bucking, shivering mackerel, eyes wide, mouths hollering silently. The boys fought off the gulls with oars, protecting their haul, greedy with excess. Then the shoal moved on, and the birds with it, and the boys sat still amid the dying fish.

'How long before they die?' Benjamin said.

'If you leave them, can be a half hour, longer sometimes.'

'They drown more slowly than us, then. What about hitting them on the head with something?'

'Hard to kill like that,' Will said. He picked one up. 'A good size. Close on a pound's weight, I'd say. Mother will be pleased. She loves mackerel.'

Slipping a finger into the fish's mouth, and with his thumb behind its head, he pulled the head back towards the body.

'Breaks their neck,' he said. 'Very quick. Best way to do it.'

So Will killed the fish and Benjamin counted them into a bucket and they stowed the oars, set the sails once again and sailed on.

As they drew closer to Shining Sands, Will's pulse quickened. You couldn't see the beach from the sea and every time he sailed there, it felt like an act of faith. Each time he left the beach he would pick out landmarks and try to stow them away in his mind for the next time: a particular bowed hawthorn on the cliff; the fall of the rocks to the water. Perhaps it was because he sailed out to the Sands too rarely, or perhaps it was some more mysterious refusal in the landscape itself, something self-protective to keep people out, but every time he returned, he felt as if he were sailing blind, no landmarks, no sign of where the Sands could be, till finally, like an ancient Greek adventurer, he must take his best guess, and turn his boat and head towards the solid rock.

'We'll row from here,' he said, letting the sails flap. 'It's always hard to find.'

'There's no beach,' Benjamin said.

'You can't see it because there's a shoal of rocks out from the shore. They look like they're part of the cliffs till you get close. A kind of optical illusion.'

Will dipped the oars: small strokes, easing closer.

'Keep your eyes skinned,' he said.

He rowed, hearing the slap of the waves beneath the boat and the high 'pheew' of a buzzard above the cliff. Then a triumphal cry.

'I've spotted it. There's a gap. Left a bit, Will, pull left.'

Gently Will rowed and the rocks opened to a channel not much wider than his oars' width. The water turned aquamarine, with sand below, and sometimes rock, and as they drew closer to the shore, the wind dropped. He rowed the boat between rock and rock and they were in.

Will gave a last, full pull, shipped the oars and the boat drifted to the shore.

'Damn, Will,' Benjamin said in a low voice. 'You didn't tell me.'

Will grinned.

'Good, eh,' he said.

Sheer cliffs rose behind, their blue-grey slate streaked with guano, and later Will would point out to Benjamin the nesting birds up there. Fine, silver shingle pitched steeply to the water, which was limpid and smooth as a lagoon. Leaping down into the shallows, Will pulled the boat up, her bow easing in with the softest sound.

'Tide's two hours past its highest now,' he said. 'We just made it in. We'll be stranded in no time. There's rocks below the water just where we came through, you'll see them then. You can't take a boat over them for long, but you get longer with a neap tide. That's why today is the perfect day for it.'

He watched Benjamin jump onto the beach and sink his hands into the sand, then lift them and let it run through his fingers. He watched him stride in great long strides, sinking with each step below the ankle so that he seemed to make a strange, slow-motion kind of progress; he watched him stride, and turn, and let out a whoop, and then another, and saw the gulls rise, startled, from their cliff. They had the whole day ahead of them, a whole day to whoop and cry, to swim, or sleep, or dream.

Will put the beer deep in a rock pool at one end of the beach. The bottles slid down the rock and sank amongst the gentle anemones. The bucket of mackerel he dug deep into the sand, covering their broken heads with an oilskin against quizzing flies, securing this with four large stones. He looked back across the beach. Benjamin stood on the groundsheet, undressing. He had spread the square of old green tarpaulin high up near the cliff and away from the water, behind the tide line, where the shingle was dry. His swimming trunks and book lay before him like sacred objects. His trousers already removed, he had his fingers round the elastic of his underpants. Will gave a low wolf whistle and Benjamin started like someone caught in some act, his hands flying to his crotch. Then he laughed, catching sight of Will in the shade, and tossed his head and pulled off his underpants in a single flourish.

The sun was high and warm, the sky clear blue. The boys laid their trousers, soaked with spray from the sailing, out to dry, then gathered driftwood. It was caught, as Will had said it would be, between the rocks that jutted down towards the water at the far end of the beach, together with all the flotsam that the sea so loves: brittle seaweed, dead birds, crab shells, cuttlefish bones, a broken buoy. Will clambered up the first reaches of the cliff and tugged out handfuls of dry grass for tinder. Then they piled the wood in the middle of the beach, tucking the grass beneath to keep it secure. Their arms and chests were scratched with their efforts; like initiation marks, Will thought, in a sacred place.

'Nothing more to do now,' he said, and somehow the saying of that made both boys abashed and they stood uncertain, looking at the water.

'Hey, look!' Will said, and he pointed to the middle distance.

Benjamin stared. 'Can't see . . .' he began, and Will threw himself and tackled Benjamin down, arms around his legs, and they rolled and struggled, pushing for purchase against the sand's shift, digging in with toes and elbows. Although Will was the slighter of the two, he had the first advantage and straddling his friend, he pinned Benjamin's arms and gripped his hips with his thighs, like a cowboy with a bucking steed.

'Solid enough, am I?' he said, wild-eyed with effort, laughing, and that set Benjamin off so he couldn't speak and tears of laughter ran down to his ears.

'Your mother didn't know you played rugby,' he said at last. 'She did look surprised.'

'You were sailing damn close to the wind,' Will said.

'But she thinks I'm a lovely boy,' Benjamin said.

'And so you are. Lovely and covered with sand.' Will let go of Benjamin's arms. 'But too gritty for any rugby playing just now.'

The sea was cold and they swam vigorously, their breath coming in short punches till their bodies grew used to it. Will lay back and floated, feeling the warmth above and the cold below, his body in two halves. He shut his eyes and listened to the hiss and chunter of the sea, the soft, grainy turn and turn about of the waves' break, and when he opened them, the world had gone to white and yellow till he gathered in his sight again. Benjamin was out already, sitting high up on the beach on the groundsheet, a towel around his waist, nose in his book.

'Hey,' Will called, but Benjamin didn't hear.

Will swam back to the shore with long, easy strokes, feeling the gentle pull of the tide against him, and stood in the shallows, looking out. He could see the shadow of the hidden rocks, the sea puckering now above them. Any minute and they would break the surface. Will raised his arm high as if a victory had been won. They were marooned, till the water rose again.

When he turned back to the beach, Benjamin was standing up and facing him. He wasn't reading any more. Will's breath quickened. With only the cap on his curly hair, Benjamin stood naked, arms by his sides, his prick high and full. He made no move, no gesture, he just stood.

Will wanted to run at him and seize him, take him in, possess him. But instead he met him in kind and walked slowly back up the beach, still wet from the sea, his skin still cold. Ten yards off he stopped and carefully he pulled off his own trunks, easing them down till they dropped to the sand. Then he turned, naked before the cliffs and rocks, before the beach and the sea and the endless tide. He felt the wind brush his cock, and at last, unable to hold himself back any longer, he went to his lover.

Gently, Benjamin lay him down and with a towel he rubbed Will's body dry. Only Will's cock he did not touch, though it rose so hard to meet him. Then he knelt, his own erection captured between his thighs, and kissed him. Softly he kissed at first, his mouth on Will's, licking the brine from his lip, then more fiercely, his tongue insistent, his teeth catching at him, wanting, hungry. He kissed Will's neck and shoulders, his ears; he kissed his small, hard nipples and bit at his hips, his thighs, and the wind blew his hair against Will's cock and Will groaned with desire.

'Fuck me,' Benjamin said, and he took Will's hands and pulled him up so that they knelt on the groundsheet, facing. Bending forward, Benjamin kissed Will on his cock's tight tip.

'Fuck me,' he said again and he smiled a knowing smile and reached over for a rucksack and pulled a jar of Vaseline from a side pocket.

'You're a thoughtful bugger,' Will said, grinning.

'Now fuck me like a dog,' Benjamin said, and Will turned him round and pushed him down. He slicked him with Vaseline, pressing, prying, so that he made his lover groan. Kneeling behind, he entered him, slowly, slowly, each thrust a little deeper, till he was in right to the hilt, possessing him.

'Feel me now,' he said, and Benjamin put his hand back to feel them joined.

Then he took hold of Benjamin's hips, pulling him close, holding him there till he came; and he yelled out, as if with one fuck there on that beach, he could make up for all the silence. And Benjamin cried out too, and they lay close for a time before making love again.

They had known of one another for four years, ever since their first arrival at the school. But for the first three and a half, placed in different forms, dormitories, sets, their paths had rarely crossed, and each was little more than a surname to the other. Will knew Benjamin as a Jew and a Londoner, attributes that could lend both suspicion and fascination to a boy in that school. Circumcisions were two a penny (there had been a vogue for them when Will was born, though Meg had resisted) but Benjamin's yarmulke – he still wore it when he first arrived – was the first Will had ever seen. As for London, Will had never visited, only listened with reluctant awe when other boys spoke of the Tube and the West End and Soho.

Still, in the last year he had become less impressed by such things than before on account of discovering the wonders of sex. Not the dark dormitory fumblings of his first years there, disavowed in the chilly light of the boarding school day, but something altogether more fun. Cross-country running; excursions into the woods to gather insects for Mr Blackman, the biology master; the long, independent study hours awarded to the senior boys; even cricket, once: all seemed organised to provide Will and his friends with time and space in which to discover the pleasures and excitements that their bodies afforded. But busy as he was with others, until that one November night, Will's glance had never stopped on Benjamin.

As for Benjamin, equally he had never given a second thought to Will; nor had he ever fumbled through his adolescence, except with himself, pinning up pictures of Audrey Hepburn and Doris Day in his mind, though it was true that they tended to meld into figures altogether more androgynous as he rose to the sticking point. But he never gave this too much thought afterwards.

All this changed for both, the evening last November that they were left behind. It was a tradition with the upper years to visit the theatre before Christmas, a two-hour journey each way by motorbus. Ice creams were bought in the interval, and on the way home fish and chips, by prior agreement with the chippie who had his heaps of battered fish and newspaper ready. Unfortunately, or so it seemed at first to them, both Benjamin and Will were ill that day with the fever that had swept through the school; and though each, separately, protested his fitness to go, each was over-ruled, and so lay that afternoon next to one another in neatly-turned sanatorium beds.

The sickness was a pleasant one, as sicknesses go, and the school nurse had seen enough of it in the last month to be familiar with its course. So she left the two boys to their own devices in the evening and went to visit her daughter in the village for an hour or two.

The boys fell to talking – the fever made it hard to read and there was little else to do – and soon found much more than a slight pleasure in each other's company. Far from finding their differences as obstacles to friendship, as they might have even a year earlier, they found them exhilarating. And although they knew how it had happened, they wondered that they had attended the same school these four years without finding one another out.

But the vital change between them occurred not in all this talk, but in the heat of fever, and it was Benjamin, all unknowing, or so he claimed later, who was responsible for it.

'There seemed nothing more natural,' he said laughing. 'I was burning up and you were shivering. It made sense to me to share the fever.'

Will was already laughing.

'It made sense to you because you were feverish,' he said. 'Delirious.'

'But it did. If you were too cold, and I was too hot, then you would cool me, and I would warm you through.'

'That's another fine mess, Stanley,' Will said, laughing so hard, he was crying. 'Best bit of sense you ever made.'

So at Benjamin's fevered bidding, Will climbed in to his bed and what began as an imagined exchange of humours – the hot for the cold – quickly became a very different kind of encounter.

Till now Will had given no thought to whom he might love. Other boys bragged of their success with girls – how far they had gone with them, mostly. Though sometimes when they talked about the future – careers and universities – they would add into the mix the kind of girl they wanted for a wife, even sometimes a particular girl. And Will would listen and agree, assuming that he must want this too. But now he had met Benjamin, he knew what he wanted, though he never dared name it, even to himself, and girls played no part in it.

'We're like Crusoe on his lonely beach,' Benjamin said. He lay back, shielding his eyes from the sun, his body soft, curved now. 'If only he and Friday . . . Would've been perfect then.'

'Or Achilles and the boy he loved,' Will said. 'What was his name? I'm famished.' He hunted in the rucksack, and then let out a whoop.

'She's put in the just-in-case food.'

'Who's Justin Case?'

'Look, Ben. Buttered bread, and more apples, and choco-late. There'll be cake somewhere. There's always cake.'

'Your mother loves you differently from Henry and Emma,' Benjamin said, running his finger softly down Will's spine.

'Not more; I don't mean that. But differently.'

'I'm older,' Will said. 'Do you want something?'

Benjamin shook his head. Will folded some bread into a sandwich and ate.

'Henry's only eleven,' he said. 'He hasn't even gone away to school yet.'

'Tell me the story you asked your mother to,' Benjamin said.

'What do you mean, she loves me differently?'

'I don't mean anything,' Benjamin said.

'But she's going to tell it tonight.'

'Tell me anyway. I want to hear you. I won't let on to her. I promise.'

'Why?'

'Please?'

'I'll tell you if . . .'

'What?'

Will laughed. 'I don't know what. I've got it all, right here and now. The whole damn lot.'

The sun was high and hot, and the boys moved the groundsheet into the shade. Benjamin fetched two bottles of beer from the rock pool and Will lay back.

'I don't remember when she first told me,' he said. 'But in the war she was on a ship sailing to marry my father in Africa and it got torpedoed. She saw lots of people die, lots of her friends, and some of them because they hadn't got their life jackets on. That's why she got so exercised about the life jackets this morning.'

'But she likes telling the story?'

'Actually not that part of it. The story she'll tell tonight will be about how she put my father's photo in one pocket and her mother's in the other when she knew the ship would sink, and that's all she arrived in Africa with; and how my father was told she was dead but wouldn't believe it and kept going back to the harbour; and how he didn't recognise her when she did arrive finally because she was so sunburnt and unwashed. They married the day after and I was born nine months after that. That's the story she'll tell tonight.'

Will stopped and thought. When he spoke again, it was haltingly. There was something he wanted to understand, but it was slippery, elusive.

'You know in the dormitory how boys would say things when the lights were out that they would never have said in the day? My mother drove me to school for my first term, and during the drive she talked, but she couldn't look at me because she was driving. So it was as if she spoke with the lights out. That's how I've always thought of it.'

'What did she tell you?'

'First off she told me she ate most of her mother's cake on the ship because she was hungry, and how sorry she was. I didn't understand everything, but I didn't want to ask in case she stopped talking. Turned on the lights. Anyway, it was the cake that got her started, and that was because of the one she'd baked me, the one in my school trunk. I'd asked her if it had cherries in it.'

'Cherries?'

'I love cherries, the sugary ones that go in cakes; so she said of course it did. And how my grandmother had put cherries in the cake she baked her for her wedding and she didn't know how she'd got hold of them, because it was the war. Anyway, the end of the cake went down with the ship and that still made her feel very sad. So I asked her why.'

'You asked her why!' Benjamin swiped him. 'You moron.'

'I was only thirteen.'

'Bet you understood soon enough, first term away at school.'

Will nodded.

'So what else did your mother tell you?'

'That the ship was full of soldiers. "Not much older than you are now," she said, and it made something go through me, don't know what it was. She'd watched the soldiers parading once; told it like it was an adventure, that she'd had to escape to do it. Climb ladders, duck under ropes. The soldiers reminded her of boys she'd known; she said one of them especially reminded her of someone.'

'Sounds like a boyfriend,' Benjamin said cautiously, 'but perhaps not your father.'

Will shrugged.

'Maybe. I don't understand why she married my father. I don't know why anybody would. But the thing was, so many of those soldiers died when the ship went down. She said one of them died leaning against her in the lifeboat. She thought he was only sleeping.

'There was a moment when she stopped the car. She'd been

talking, telling me all of this. But then she stopped the car and turned round and put her hand on the back of my neck. It was quite strange. She hadn't done anything like that since I was about five. It tickled a bit. It felt as if she was trying to get hold of my hair, but I'd been to the barber's the day before, so there was nothing there. Anyway, she turned and she said: "The people you love, they just slip away. There one minute, gone the next. I won't let you do that, William." She was so fierce. I remember those words exactly. But whenever I think about it, I don't know who she was talking to, or what she was talking about.'

Will fell silent, then stood up, dizzy with telling. Benjamin put on his trunks and piled the driftwood into a bonfire.

'Didn't feel safe, lighting a fire without them on,' he said.

Will laughed. He fetched four mackerel and put them on the griddle, nose to tail. He pushed the dry grass underneath Ben's pile, making sure it had enough air and enough small driftwood to catch to. He wouldn't have built the bonfire this way, but he was happy. From the rucksack he took out his cigarette lighter and a penknife. The penknife was looped onto a string and Will put it around his neck so that it hung on his chest like a medal.

'Fine lighter,' Benjamin said. 'A lover's gift?'

He lit the fire and the driftwood, dry as bones, blazed at once. The flames were invisible in the sun, like ghosts in the air. But the heat they put up was ferocious, and the boys stepped back to watch.

'Once it's died back we can cook the fish,' Will said.

'Patroclus,' Benjamin said. 'He was the one Achilles loved.'

Stropping the penknife blade on a stone, Will picked up the first fish and with a soft stroke, he slit it gills to tail. Then two cuts top and bottom, and he slipped his fingers into its belly, tugged out the innards and threw them on the fire. Swiftly he gutted the other three.

Benjamin said: 'What will happen? We haven't got a battle to disguise things and anyway, England isn't Greece. Your mother hopes you might meet a nice girl at the dance.'

'My mother likes you, Ben.'

'She wouldn't like me so much if she'd seen us on this beach.'

Will stood, cradling the fish in his hands.

'Need the water,' he said.

The boys walked down to the falling sea. The sand was packed and dark underfoot. Will rinsed the fish, swirling them to and fro, and their bodies muddied the water for a moment.

'I don't know,' Will said. 'I don't know what will happen.'

The flames had died back now and Will made a level place for the griddle. Carefully he laid out the fish.

'Why can't we go on as we are?' he said. 'Go to university. Get jobs. You want to be a lawyer, follow your father. I don't know what I'll do. Something unlike mine.'

'I think your mother wants you to break the mould,' Benjamin said. 'Do something daring, or inventive. She'd be disappointed if you followed your father.'

'So why don't we do that?' Will said. 'And we can share a flat, have our own kind of life.'

'But she doesn't want you to break that kind of mould. Your mother can't order you to dances forever, but she's no fool.'

'But she doesn't want me to disappear,' Will said. 'And I would if I did as she asked. Found a girl, got married. I'd be like these fish, just the shape left, just some flesh, but no heart, no guts.'

Using two small stones, Will turned the fish on their rack.

'Don't your parents want you to marry a nice Jewish girl?' he said.

'Eventually, I suppose. But my brother's done it already; it's taken the heat off.'

They talked on a little till the fish were cooked, their electric blue skins blackened and the flesh turned grey. But the discussion had run its usual course and both were relieved to stop. They ate – mackerel and sandwiches, apples and cake – both boys famished, eager to fill their senses with what was here and what was now, to push away the smell of the future. The mackerel was as delicious as hunger and fire could make it, and after they had eaten their fill, they made love gently. Then Benjamin read his book, and Will lay beside him, curled against his lover's thigh. His limbs felt heavy, his mind drifted, and soon he slept.

He woke with a start. The air had changed. Benjamin had placed a sweater over him as he slept but still he felt cold. The wind was gusting fitfully, chopping at the water first here and then there. Benjamin stood staring at it. The sun still shone, but hazily, as though something were draped over it, like a piece of the muslin his mother used for making marmalade.

He looked out to the shoal of rocks. There was no question that they looked less distinct. But he didn't want to give up the languor of their day just yet and he glanced at Benjamin, standing there in just his shirt and sweater. It would only get colder now, though, and the fret would get denser, and after a minute he stood up and got dressed.

He called out. 'Sea fret. We'll have to go, soon as we can. You remember, the old man?'

Benjamin turned, as if from a revery, his thoughts still drifting on the water.

'But you said there wouldn't be one.'

Will shrugged. 'I was wrong. It's OK. We'll be out of here as soon as the tide's high enough. Shouldn't be too bad. And we'll keep close to the shore heading back. Once we're round the point and in to the estuary, we're home and dry.'

Benjamin gathered up the gear while Will gutted and sluiced off the remaining mackerel.

'She'll be pleased,' he said, wanting to reassure. 'Plenty for supper.'

'It's safe, though?' Benjamin said. And with a stab at the jocular: 'After all, we haven't got an *A to Z*. It's the only way I can find my way anywhere.'

'I've been in one of these before,' Will said. 'They can come in very fast, take you by surprise. But I do know what to do.'

Benjamin nodded. 'OK.'

'We'll put on the oilskins now, and cap and plimsolls.'

'They're sodden,' Benjamin said.

'Keep your feet warmer than nothing at all,' Will said, but

Benjamin drew the line at soggy plimsolls, and wouldn't wear the damp cap either.

'If you catch a chill, my mother will blame me,' Will said.

'And she'll be right.' Benjamin's voice was partly amused and partly not.

By the time the tide was high enough for the boys to leave, the fret had grown denser. Will rowed them through the channel and into the open sea and within moments the beach, the rocks, the very land had disappeared and he could see no further than three pulls of the oar. They were no distance away and yet it was as if nothing else existed in the world beyond this boat in its circle of water. Everything was silenced: gulls, wind, even somehow the noise from the oars. They dipped and rose into a silent sea.

The fret was set right in now, a wetness in the air that was not rain and yet it had soaked Will's trousers and was gathered in Benjamin's hair like a spray of dull stars.

Will said: 'You watch for the shore, call out when you see land, and I'll take care of the sailing. We'll inch our way home.'

'But we can't see anything. What about rocks?'

'There's only the Brigstone,' Will said. 'We won't be going near her.'

Will could hear fear in Benjamin's voice, but he made no acknowledgement of it. That would help neither of them right now. As for his own fear, his own feelings, he kept these to himself too. Benjamin was right. He had been complacent, and arrogant. The fret had been forecast; he'd been warned. But he'd lied to his mother, and brushed off the old man.

He'd thought the gods would keep the sun blazing because he wanted it; because this was to be their perfect day. And he had so nearly got away with it.

Slowly, slowly they felt their way up the coast, tacking out from the shore and in again. Out for the count of twenty, and in; out again and in. The wind was erratic and Will sailed with all the wit he knew to keep their course. They must stay close, but not too close or they'd fall foul of the rocks that hid below the surface, ready and eager to hole a small boat like theirs, for all Will's easy words. Too far out – and it might be no more than a handful of yards – and they could be swallowed up by the fret and lost.

'Call out when you see land,' Will said. 'Eyes skinned, or we'll be on the rocks.'

He worked hard to keep his voice calm and to seem unafraid, but somehow he betrayed himself and he knew there would be a reckoning later. And he made each starboard tack with his heart in his mouth till Benjamin called 'Land' again.

Still the fret was thick around them so that they could see and hear only each other. Once there was the sound of an outboard engine, a deep chug chug that came from nowhere and went to nowhere, but they never had sight of the boat; and once, as they came close to the invisible shore, Benjamin shouted 'Seal,' and as they went about Will saw something sleek and dark and silent slip down into the sea.

How long they sailed like this for, Will didn't know, the only sounds Benjamin's cry of 'Land' and then, fast on it, his own 'Ready about'. It seemed hours. A cramping had started in his rudder arm and he could feel the strain behind his eyes. His body felt tight as if he might snap suddenly, like a rubber band pulled too far beyond its limit. Finally, as the starboard tack grew longer and the wind dropped, he knew they had reached the mouth of the estuary.

'Safe now,' he called to Benjamin.

As the estuary narrowed, it became easier to navigate. Trees loomed on one side, dripping green. Will dropped the sails and rowed. It was slower, and safer with all the yachts and small boats moored.

'Can you tie up somewhere for a minute before we get back?' Benjamin said.

'Here, do you mean? In the estuary?'

'Anywhere.'

So Will caught the next buoy and looped the painter through the ring.

'There,' he said. He rolled his shoulders round, feeling them ease.

Benjamin faced him square.

'You shouldn't have done that,' he said slowly.

Will was perplexed.

'We're back, Ben. Safe. I got us back.'

'I'm going to make a speech, because I don't know how else to make you understand.'

'I know you're angry about the weather,' Will said, 'but it happens at sea.'

'What if you hadn't got away with it? If we hadn't found our way home?'

'But we did.'

'You can't always just wish and make things so. This trip. Our perfect day. Your life. You were as scared as I was out there. You knew better than me how dangerous it was, and it was your fault.'

'I'm sorry . . .' Will began, but Benjamin waved it away.

'I told you it was a speech,' he said.

Will stared at the buoy they had tied to, its dull, dented silver slick with seaweed, crusted with barnacles. It might have floated there all his life, longer, impervious to the tides, impervious to the weather, rocking steady.

'I've been lucky so far,' Benjamin said, 'but life doesn't owe me anything. So I'm going to make it go on giving me what I want. I'm going to work, and study, and battle for things. I want to battle for you, Will. With my family, with yours, do whatever it takes. But you need to battle too. What if we had lost the land? Everything's not a bloody game. *This* isn't a game. We're not playing at boats in the bath; we're not playing Roundheads and bloody Cavaliers any more.'

Sound carries over water, but Benjamin spoke his piece quietly. Then – 'I've finished,' he said. 'I know you're different to me, and I know you're sorry, and we did have a perfect day till it changed. Just tell me you'll take more care next time.'

Much later Will tried to recall what he'd said then. Enough, and seriously spoken, that they'd made up and kissed out there, hidden inside the wet air. Then untied and gone on.

Soon after they passed close enough to a yacht, that Will could read her name.

'The *Aurora*,' he said. 'We're nearly back. Look out for the jetty. It's got Estuary Hotel on a sign. Our slipway's just to the right.'

And they were there, drifting up so quiet and calm.

He shipped the oars and jumped out.

'Come on,' he said with a grin. 'Think of the hot muffins. Think of the warm bath.'

'Typical of you. Stomach first.'

Benjamin stepped out gingerly and together they brought the trailer down, easing it into the water and under the dinghy, bringing her bow high before they pulled her out.

'Plain sailing from here,' Will said. 'Clean her up, stow the sails, pack away the gear; just the walk then, and we can't get lost.'

He gave the boat a pat, because she had done well by him, and in the end he had done well by her.

They pulled the trailer up the slope and on to the track, one hand each on the trailer head, the other gripping the boat edge. Benjamin's fingers were white with cold and his lips were pale.

'I don't need the muffin, but you need the warm bath,' Will said.

'Enough sailing for a while,' Benjamin said, but he was smiling.

Along the track they pulled the boat, and they were almost there, almost back.

It came from nowhere, it came from the air and exploded through him, a bolt, a silent force, a terrible shaft of electricity that hurled him away from the boat and slammed him into the ground, into the thicket of weeds alongside the track. He was burning, he felt he was burning, and everything was white . . .

. . . His eyes hurt. Why did his eyes hurt? And his hands, and his feet; somebody was groaning. He opened his eyes and slowly the light resolved to grey. Had he been sleeping? He had been somewhere. The mast of a boat struck up at an angle above him, and beyond it a thick black line ran across the sky. He couldn't think where he was. It was cold on this ground but he felt very hot. A single thought came, that he should move. Slowly he tried out his arms and legs, and there was the groaning again. He was lying, he found, in a twist, one leg flung across the other, one arm over his head, one under his back.

He tried to bring his arms back to himself, though the pain in his hands was very strong. Eventually he was able to roll onto his stomach, and then he saw the belly of a boat, and beyond it, another boy lying.

Knowledge came like a cold wave.

'Ben,' he called, but his voice was small and Benjamin didn't hear him.

It took Will forever to reach him, digging at the ground with his elbows, his shoulders screaming. Behind him, his legs dragged like dead wood and his feet burned. Benjamin lay on his back, his cold, bare toes pointing upwards, and on each toe was a blood-red blister. He had one arm by his side and there, too, in the palm of his hand, a small red circle, as if someone had pressed a hot coin on him. His eyes were closed and his mouth was curled in a slight smile, for all the world as if he were simply sleeping for a while in the weeds beside the track in the cold, wet air.

Later Will saw it, burnt into his retina: an arc of light, a shaft of brutal, pointed energy.

'Ben,' he said and he bent forward to feel Benjamin's breath, or, if he could only make his fingers work, to find the jump of a pulse in his neck. If he could only make his fingers work. Then awkward in his own pain, he took his lover in his arms and tried to keep him warm.

He didn't remember being found. Had no recollection of his father bending to him, or of his mother's hands around his shoulders, on his hair. He didn't feel the passing touch of the St Christopher medal she wore around her neck. He didn't see their faces when they touched Benjamin's cheek, or hear their shouts for help, or see others come running. It took two of them to prise his arms away, and carry him down the track, a dead weight.

So he didn't hear his mother's cry that Benjamin was still warm – quick – a doctor – quick. Because if he had been there he could have told her that it was only borrowed warmth, and why else had *he* held him so tight all that time? Nor did he see the doctor crouch in the weeds, nor see his fist thump down onto his lover's chest, once, twice, a third time; nor hear the man's cry of horror, for all his years at work with death, when from Benjamin's mouth came, dark and clotted, all the stuff of his life.

Will had gone away in his head for a time.

When at last he came back, it was to a white bed where he lay and lay, his body screaming at him, and his mind.

His mother came and he saw in her face what he knew already.

She said: 'It was his heart that killed him.'

He said: 'Oh.' He didn't say: Well, I knew that. I didn't need to be told. He didn't say that out loud, not to his mother, not to anyone. And she never told him what she had seen with the doctor. She never told anyone that.

She brought flowers from the garden and muffins and books gathered from his room. He didn't tell her that one of the books was Benjamin's.

'How do you feel?' she said.

He shrugged.

'Does it hurt?'

'Do you mean my hands and my feet?' he said. Do you mean my head and my heart and my flesh and my bones?

Meg walked over to the window. Will's eyes were sore and so the curtains were drawn, but the sun was pushing at them, shoving fingers round the edge. She shook them wide shut again with a practised air.

Stigmata, he thought. Hands, feet, heart. Benjamin, my Jewish boy, you would have found that funny.

'The doctors say you might not need a skin graft. And they say the headaches and dizziness will pass.'

'I brought us back safe,' Will said.

'The doctors say you were very lucky.'

'I lost him, Mother.'

'I understand.'

'No, you don't. I loved him, and I brought him back safe,

but I've lost him.'

Meg sat on the bed beside him.

'I had a brother who was lost,' she said, but she didn't say more, and he didn't ask her, not then.

She stood up again. 'The little ones want to come and see you. I said perhaps in a couple of days, depending how you feel.'

'Henry will ask me questions. He'll try not to but he won't be able to stop it.'

'Emma cries when I mention you. They are very sad about Benjamin. It would help her; it would reassure her.'

'Bring Emma,' he said. 'I'd like to see Emma.'

After his mother had gone he slept again, for an hour or a day, he didn't know, sometimes drifting deep, sometimes waking as nurses came and went. Once he woke to find a doctor showing him off, others around the bed noting him, pointing. The doctor spoke of ferning patterns and of cutaneous burns; he counted out Will's burnt toes, eenie, meenie, minie, mo; and as they turned to leave he spoke more quietly and in a different voice, of congestive heart failure and haemorrhaged lungs, and Will shut his eyes against the light again.

'Did they do an autopsy?' he said.

His mother was putting more flowers in a vase.

'William, he was buried yesterday.'

'I know. You told me, and Father was to attend; he didn't like Benjamin.'

'He was there for all of us.'

'But did they do an autopsy first?' he said.

'Please, Will,' Meg said. She got up and stood at the window, though there was nowhere to see with the curtain still shrouding it. 'I don't want to think about it.'

'Did they?' he said.

'They have to,' she said finally. 'The law.'

So they'd cut him open. Easy as cleaning a fish. Run a knife down that beautiful chest, followed that delicate line of dark hair down and down with their keen blade, split wide his stomach and dabbled about. Dabbled about in his boy, then zipped him up again and buried him.

'They think it was his finger on the halyard. The coroner is guessing from the burn,' she said.

'Was it sunny?' Will said.

'Sunny?'

'When they buried him. Was the sun shining?'

'I don't know, Will. The funeral was in London.'

'The sun should be shining. It shone all that day till the fret.'

'I'll ask your father how it was.'

'I know what they do. He told me after his grandfather's funeral. The body should be guarded and honoured, watched over by those who love him until it is buried. And when it is buried, everybody puts a spade of earth over the coffin. Father will have done it.'

'He'll have done it from you too. From us all. Benjamin's family knew you couldn't be there.'

'And afterwards you're not supposed to shave for a week, or look in mirrors.'

'I'll bring Emma tomorrow,' his mother said.

So the next day his little sister came. She had a doll in a small basket that she placed carefully at the end of the bed.

'What are you doing?' he said.

'Mother said I should bring something to play with in case you were asleep.'

'I didn't know you had a doll,' Will said. 'I thought you didn't like them very much.'

'I'm practising to do it better.'

'To do what better?' Will asked.

'Play with dolls better. It's done a lot at school.'

'Ah,' Will said. He was, he realised, very glad to see his sister.

'And Mother will be back in an hour and I'm to be quiet if you're tired, and practise, and just-wait-patiently.'

'There's a special chair for visitors,' Will said, 'or you can come and sit on the bed, beside me.'

He watched her consider this, and then she took the chair, scrambling a little to gain the seat. She wriggled to get comfortable and put a hand on each knee. Then she turned to Will.

'Why did it get Benjamin and not you?' she said.

'Mother said you'd been very upset.'

'Benjamin is funny,' she said. 'I don't want him to be dead.'

'I don't know why,' Will said. 'I don't know why it left me here.'

'But there wasn't any lightning,' Emma said.

'No,' Will said. 'No thunder, no lightning.'

'Father says he's going to sell the land, and we're not allowed to go there any more.'

She looked at his feet. Sitting on the chair, she wasn't much taller than the high hospital bed.

'Did it burn all your toes?' she said.

He nodded.

'Each one?'

'Each one,' he said.

'Like the Pobble,' she said, and then: 'And are you very sad about Benjamin? Very very sad?'

Will turned away a little. He hadn't cried till now.

'Mary's my best friend,' Emma said. 'Mary Angela Dawkins.'

She shuffled forward in the seat so she could swing her legs, watching them to and fro.

'And I know it wasn't lightning, but if she got struck by lightning, then I'd be very, very sad, and she said I could have her china tea service; and if I was, then she could have my doll, but that's not as special because she has a doll already.'

She looked up at Will.

'But she doesn't like boats or adventures,' she said, 'so I don't either.'

He felt each upswing of her foot, its gentle brush against the bed. He understood her and he wanted to tell her that they'd been safe home, that Benjamin didn't die because of him, but he said only: 'As long as she's a nice friend.'

'Don't cry, Will,' she said and she took out a handkerchief. 'I brought it specially.'

Will took it in his bandaged hands and patted at his cheeks.

'Anyway, Mary said girls had friends and boys had chums, so Benjamin was your best chum,' and Will smiled despite himself because she said it as though this might change something.

'Mary has very definite opinions,' he said.

She took the handkerchief back, folded it and put it in her pocket.

'She is nearly seven and a half,' she said with the air of someone who knows that the six months makes all the difference.

'Ah.'

'Benjamin was your best chum, wasn't he?' Emma said, needed, Will realised, formal clarification of their status.

'Yes, he was my best chum,' he said, and they were both silent for a while, she swinging her legs, he hit with the memory of Benjamin's sleeping face.

'I'm going to get down for a bit and practise with my doll,' she said.

He watched her pick the doll out of the basket and cradle it in her arms. She rocked it to and fro several times, then appeared to adjust its frock, rub at some mark on its cheek before depositing it back in the basket and tucking it in again.

'There,' she said, and returned to her seat.

Pain came in waves. It was worst in his chest, but he didn't want to give it too much room. He had cleaned the mackerel that day, then flipped the blade inside and hung the penknife on its string around his neck. Safe, careful. But when the electricity bolt struck, the knife had scored its own mark against his ribs, an oval of charred skin that the nurses dressed each day, although the burn pain – searing, aching – was not so much there as all around it, up to his heart and down to his navel.

The doctor had explained to his mother why this was and she'd told him.

'There are no nerves left where the worst burns are; so where you feel the pain, that's around the edges, where the burn is less bad.'

He didn't want to cry out, or groan, because it would frighten Emma and she might not want to visit again.

'What shall I do, Emma?' he said, because if he could listen to what she said, then he could ignore the pain, or pretend to. And besides, she might know the answer as well as anyone.

Emma leaned forward, put her elbows on the bed and rested her head, thinking.

'Father said when he was sad, he did more work, but he didn't say why. And when Muftie died, I cried. But Father said I oughtn't too much, because rabbits can't be your best friend or your best chum because they're only animals.'

'No,' Will said.

They were each silent for a minute, each caught by a different kind of loss. Will rested his bandaged hand gently on her head.

'Your hair is so cool,' he said, and she giggled.

'Hair isn't cool or hot, silly,' she said. 'Besides, you can't feel it with all the bandages.'

'Why don't you be my best chum now?' Will said.

She lifted her head and looked at him. His face was serious.

'No, sisters can't be,' she said and then: 'Did you know that Barbara Lavery has been to our house twice? She was very sorry that you couldn't go to her birthday party.'

'I don't know Barbara Lavery,' Will said. 'I've barely seen her since I was little.'

'She's very nice and very pretty,' Emma said, 'and she was very sorry. Mother made her tea both times and the second time there was cake.'

Pain burned in his chest and he closed his eyes to meet it. His anger rose and he spat the words out like grit: 'Well, if Mother gave her cake, then she can be my best chum now.' But when he opened his eyes again, Emma had got down and she was tugging at the chair.

'I'm going to look out of the window,' she said and he heard the shake in her voice.

He waited while she positioned the chair and fetched her doll, then kneeled up to look out, only her legs and her shoe soles visible to him now, hidden as she was behind the curtain. Then he spoke gently. 'Emma, I wasn't angry; not with you.'

She didn't reply, and he tried again.

'It hurts,' he said. 'Everything is painful and sometimes I can't keep it in.'

The legs shuffled. He heard her point things out to the doll – the flowerbed, a nurse, a tree. Then, in a small voice: 'When you're not so sad, maybe you could have a new chum.'

'Yes,' he said. 'That's right.'

His father visited at the weekend. The last time, a week earlier, Will had been asleep when he came and it was only from the sharp smell of his cologne that Will knew he had been there. This time George nodded and patted Will on the shoulder and muttered something, Will wasn't sure what. Something like 'Glad . . . jolly good . . . fine recovery.' Then his father sat down in the chair and opened a notebook.

'Meeting with Messrs Gladstone and Gladstone regarding land adjoining hotel,' he said. 'Thought you might like to know the outcome.'

This offering of information, man to man, was as close as his father would come to expressing affection and Will said: 'Yes, I'd like to know,' which wasn't strictly true. He didn't want to think about that strip of land; it ran alongside his dreams too much already. But he did want to know that his father had got him in mind somewhere.

George read out what he'd written down, speaking in notes, as if whole sentences were an indulgence:

'Discussions with the hotel. I'll sell land if they'll make sure never used for storing boats again. Make sure it's safe.'

Will thought: Somewhere in there he is sorry for me and angry and doing whatever he can do. But there is nothing he can do, because what can anybody do now?

'Freak thing,' his father went on. 'Sea fret. Mast. Ten feet between. Spoken to several people. Authorities. Freak thing.'

Then he read from the notebook again.

'If hotel was cottage, you'd have been fine. Only 11,000 volts. Just some burns, if anything. But line to hotel carries 33,000 volts. Electricity found the mast, carried in the fret. Corona effect.'

'And crowned Ben,' Will said.

'Found your friend,' George said.

'Know thine enemies,' Will said. 'You always told me to do that. Always seemed like good advice. But not this time.'

George checked his watch and stood up.

'Must talk about your future. Once you're home. Glad you're feeling better.'

The nurses came and went and his body began to heal. Soon he could go home, they said, as long as his wounds were dressed each day. He couldn't see his chest or his feet, but he had watched as they dealt with his hands. The new skin would be puckered, they said; there would be scars, and he nodded: of course.

Emma came again, with Henry this time, and they brought Monopoly to play, unfolding the board precariously on Will's legs. Will didn't like the game, but he was pleased to see them and so they played for a while. Emma was too young to understand its ruthless economics and insisted on buying properties by card colour – she liked the orange and the red ones, but not the blue, or green, and certainly not the stations; Henry had his father's shrewd eye, playing the percentage game, and Will didn't care. So after a time the game descended into anarchy, and Will declared Henry the winner and sent himself to gaol forever, which made Emma laugh. Will played and joked and didn't mention Benjamin, and his grief was hidden inside him like a stone.

They sent him home two days later and he walked from the hospital like an old man, hobbling, exhausted. The day was sunny and the bright light startled him. They'd had to prise his arms away from Benjamin when they found him, but now he hadn't the strength of a child.

'Mother,' he said, his voice urgent, but when she answered him, he couldn't name his fear, and he just shrugged. 'Thought I'd left something behind,' he said.

Meg drove the car gently, easing round the deep Devonian corners, taking the longer route home around the cliff to avoid any well-wishers greeting them in the village. Will saw this, was relieved, and though he knew she didn't intend it, he felt the obligation: to behave right in return, to dance the dance.

He was so angry and he wanted to hurt her. Smash her with his fist, wound her with his grief. He wanted her there, and he wished she would leave him alone.

'I've made a nice tea,' Meg said. 'The little ones are excited. They're making a list of games already, I should warn you.'

Will looked out of the window. The hedgerows looked the same, only darker. The Lady's Bedstraw still flowered and he could still pluck it if he chose.

'I'd like to sleep in the spare room for a bit,' he said.

'I had wondered,' Meg said. 'The bed is made up.'

Because, he thought, if he lived as a stranger to himself, then perhaps he would manage. An idea came to him, returned rather. He would say it out loud now, see how it sounded; how she took it, and how he did, before they were home, before they were anywhere.

He looked round at his mother.

'I've come to a decision,' he said.

He tried to make his tone light, but it was hard and flat and he saw the anxiety on his mother's face.

'I'm going to take Emma's advice,' he said.

'Emma's advice?' Meg expression softened. 'What did she advise you to do?'

'Now Benjamin is dead, I'm going to invite Barbara Lavery to be my chum.'

Meg slowed into a bend.

'Do you mean,' she said, 'that Emma advised you to marry Barbara?'

'She advised me to be her chum.'

'You might say that amounts to the same thing, coming from your seven-year-old sister.' His mother's voice was amused, but curt.

'Emma's a good judge of character,' Will said. 'Much better than Henry.'

'You are joking, Will?' There was a note of concern now in his mother's voice, as if she couldn't tell now what to take seriously and what not. 'You don't even know the girl, not since you grew up anyway.'

'I don't know what a joke is,' he said. 'But Emma said Barbara had been round twice and that you'd given her cake.'

'She's a nice girl, and she was concerned,' Meg said. 'You – Benjamin – it cast something of a pall over her birthday.'

So his mother was sorry for her. That was it.

'Christ, Mother!' he said. 'I'm sorry for the pall we've cast. Very, very sorry!'

Meg stopped the car, dead, in the middle of the lane and turned round to face him.

'Could have gone through the windscreen then,' he said,

and he heard the sarcasm in his voice, but he couldn't help it.

'Look at me,' she said once and before he'd had time to do so, again: 'Look at me!'

He twisted in his seat, nursing his bandaged hands to him in what he knew, as he did it, was a deliberate gesture; a gesture that said: these wounds, these are my weapons and my defence. But she looked only at his face and refused to see them.

'Benjamin was a close friend,' Meg said, 'and grieving takes its own time. I know you're in shock. The doctor said they think that it can stay in the body – in the actual tissue, in the bloodstream – for months. But even so, I don't want to hear language like that from my son.'

The lane reared up on either side of them, the green so high it blotted out the sun. Love or no love, Will thought.

'I apologise,' he said. 'It must be the shock speaking,' but he said the words gently, so she would believe him.

'And still, that's no reason to be uncivil and I'm glad the little ones aren't in the car to hear you, your tone as much as your words. Perhaps Emma is right and Barbara would be good for you. But if you do invite her, then do so because you'd like to see her. Don't invite her otherwise.'

It was quite a speech from his mother. He thought she might put her hand to his head after this, stroke his hair. He hoped she would, despite himself. But she put the car back into gear and drove on. Will didn't look at her, but he could see, out of the corner of his eye, that she was thinking about something.

'The day you sailed to Shining Sands,' she said finally, 'I was cross with you about something. Do you remember?'

Will nodded. Of course he remembered. That morning, that day, every last detail, was carved into him. His beloved Ben, curled around his sleep, so ready to be woken. His mother telling him to live a life of his own making.

'That hasn't changed,' she said. 'Benjamin's death hasn't changed it.'

The mornings came, each of them, like a terrible reprise. The summer stayed warm and bright and the sun shone through the curtains like a punishment. Will slept sparely in the spare bed, often woken by dream fits of jagged colour or fearful journeys that swung relentlessly into catastrophe, and from which he lurched awake, sweating, heart racing. He came to dread sleep and would stay awake as long as he could, or take a sleeping bag into his sister's room. It was better there where he could hear Emma's easy breathing, though his parents disapproved.

But gradually his body mended, his strength returned and even his sleep settled. In the following weeks the dressings came off one by one, first from each toe, then his chest and finally his hands. He made a game of it with Emma, counting his body back into life, like one of the number rhymes she pooh-poohed now she was so grandly six. Before he would have sailed, or swum, every day in a summer like this; now he didn't once go near the sea.

He saw Benjamin everywhere: at the turn of the stair, or snugged into the heap of sleeping bag. He glimpsed him at the twist of the lane, the cap on his head, and shouted out and ran down; and once he heard Benjamin, he knew he had, talking to his mother in the greenhouse. So he crept up and listened. He was right, his mother was speaking and not to herself, but no one answered her. And when he came round the corner silently and stood in the doorway, she didn't see him for a minute, so he listened to her talk, quite plainly, to a boy, or a man, who wasn't there. She jumped when she saw him, and shouted his name: 'Will!' But she didn't explain, and he thought only: I'm not alone, seeing ghosts.

He wasn't sure why he asked Barbara to tea finally. It wasn't because he thought they'd be friends, and he certainly didn't feel his mother's sense of duty. Perhaps, like sleeping in the spare room, it was in the effort to live as a stranger; or perhaps he simply wanted to confound himself.

She came and she was very real. A girl his own age with thick, dark hair wound up on her head, and a handbag, and a cardigan the colour of an orange sunset. She ate cake, was charming with his mother, playful with Emma and serious with Henry, discussing quite readily the finer points of cricket, so that Henry declared her afterwards to be the best sort of a girl. And with Will she was reserved, respectful, funny, so that despite himself, he found that he liked her.

The second time Will invited her to the house, he did so when he knew they would be alone. They sat in the garden, backs up against a tree, and talked.

'You know, I was planning an escape from your birthday party,' Will said. 'I don't like dances and Mother was insisting.'

'I wish you could have come, and made your escape,' she said. 'You and your friend, both.'

'You'd have liked Benjamin,' Will said. 'He was nicer than me.'

She smoked a cigarette, leaning in towards him to light it from his lighter. She was a good listener and she didn't try to gainsay, or commiserate, or reassure. She leaned against the tree, her skirts pulled down between her knees, her fingers weaving and unweaving the edges of her scarf.

So Will talked on that afternoon, as he hadn't been able to with anyone else. He described Benjamin for her: what he looked like, how he laughed, what made him angry, how he died. He told her about their perfect day, enough of it at least that she'd understand.

'He was my closest friend,' Will said. 'I don't know how to . . .'

He didn't know whether she understood what he didn't say. It was never named, not by him and not by her. But she listened, and he felt less alone.

The summer was nearly over and both would soon return to school for a final year. In the last week of the holiday they met every day. She told him her dreams and her plans and the arguments she had with her mother; she made him laugh with her dislike of boats, and horses, and walks, and she told of how she longed for the city.

'We were going to share a flat in the city, Benjamin and me,' Will said. 'And maybe go to India.' Live unsuitably, he thought, God knows I wanted to do that.

'What did your parents think?'

'My father is relieved now, though he can't say that, can't speak ill. But he didn't like Benjamin. Too clever. "That Jewish boy", he called him once. And he didn't trust us together. We might have done anything.'

Once they took the bus into town and saw a film and on the way back she took his hand and stroked its puckered palm. They kissed too, not quite chaste, not quite not.

He didn't know what he felt; hunger for another human body, affection, perhaps even desire. He didn't know what was assumed between them; wasn't sure for himself.

'We'll write?' he said.

'Perhaps.'

When he returned to school, Will buried himself deep as he could. For a few days there was a flurry of excitement, a quizzing curiosity, about Benjamin's death. But once that died down, he was left alone with his grief and his puzzlement. He had meant it as a joke, when he first invited Barbara for tea, an angry unspoken joke with his mother, but his sister had been right and they were chums now. More than. He wrote to Barbara, long letters full of observations and a curiosity that was partly willed and partly real. He talked of his ambitions and his intentions; he spoke of his desire to see her again, and he made little mention of Benjamin. Sometimes she didn't reply and sometimes she did: short letters that shifted between impersonal affection, as though copied direct from some template, and bewilderment. What were they to each other? More than friends and less than lovers, like their kiss.

It was winter, nearly Christmas, and the bedroom was cold and the day still dark outside. Will heard his father's heavy steps on the stairs, the slam of the bathroom door, the crunch of the key in the lock. Beneath the covers, he was warm, his body weightless. He ran his fingers over his ribs, feeling the tight, smooth surface of the scar, the 'not there' touch that still disturbed him, where the nerves had been burnt off.

'I feel queasy,' he said. 'It's the first time I've seen her since the summer.'

He kept his voice low; Emma had already asked him who he talked to in his bedroom and he told her she shouldn't be listening, and he made a monster face at her, but he spoke to Benjamin very quietly after that.

'I miss you. I wake up and I miss you,' he said.

Out of bed, he switched on the bar heater and stood shivering, thinking, before its building heat.

'She knows about you. You and me. I'm sure she does. I didn't tell her that, not directly, but she knows it. So if she still wants to see me?'

Then he gathered himself together and dressed and went downstairs.

In the kitchen his mother was rolling pastry. The air was warm and sweet-smelling. She looked up.

'How's the Pobble?' she said.

'I can feel them today. Where's Father?'

'Gone for the Sunday papers,' she said. 'It's today, isn't it? That you're seeing Barbara?'

'First time since September.'

'Because I'd like to say something now, before George is back.'

Will waited. She punched out some more pastry disks, gathered the tatters into a ball, and came and sat down opposite.

'I'll be blunt,' she said.

Will looked at her hands, noticed how the flour picked out the hairs along her fingers. She rapped her fingers on the table, making a little flour cloud.

'Don't do something you'll regret,' she said.

'I've done that already.' The words came out before he could think. And when his mother raised her eyes in a question he added: 'I did that on a day in July.'

'Ah . . .' she said, and he held his breath and wondered whether he had said too much. Because for all that she had liked Benjamin, and was horrified by his death, and had grieved for her son grieving, he was sure she'd have no tolerance for their love.

'I'm sorry, Mother. Tell me what I'd regret,' he said, unable to keep the bitterness from his tongue.

'Barbara seems like a lovely girl, and nothing would make me happier. But don't marry too quickly. Don't marry because you think you ought. That's what you'd regret.'

He breathed out. He had still supposed, he didn't know why, that she was going to say something about Benjamin, perhaps because it was so much in his mind. But for her to talk of marriage was absurd.

'Mother, I'm home from school. Two terms yet before I leave, even. Then I'm going to university.'

'Still, don't,' she said.

'We're going for a walk. Nothing more.'

She handed him a wooden spoon and pointed to the mixing bowl. 'Stir, and wish. I've waited for you.'

He turned the heavy mixture over and over, catching the glint of the sixpence once, smelling the sweet cinnamon and the nutmeg must, and closed his eyes and wished.

'It can be lonely in a marriage, too. And she is not to toy with,' Meg said.

'I like her. That's all.'

'You barely know her. And you're still grieving. I'm glad something good, or someone, has come out of all this. But don't use her, Will.'

'There are boys at school who talk of marriage,' he said.

'Don't talk to me of boys,' his mother said, and her sharp tone surprised him. 'They're no more than that. Just boys.'

He walked with Barbara along the winter lanes, keeping away from the sea, and they held hands, glove to glove. And talked, carefully, wonderingly, because there seemed to be so much at stake, so fast.

'You never speak of Benjamin now,' she said.

He swiped a stick at the high hawthorn hedge, sent down a shower of drops.

'I don't know how to,' he said. 'Though I had a disagreement with my mother just this morning, as a matter of fact.'

He knew he didn't love this girl as he had loved that boy. He had no wish to consume her, to ravish or command her. He didn't long for her fingers on his skin, didn't long to kiss her. She was the price of his guilt, she was his retribution. He had a love and he let him die; he must pay now and love against his nature. Yet he hadn't lied when he spoke to his mother. He liked Barbara, maybe more than liked her. And she was his defence against grief.

It was New Year's Eve when giggling and a little drunk, they ran away from the party before midnight, climbing from the cloakroom window. It was cold and clear, that last night of the old year. Will stood on the frosted grass, leaned his head back and yelled up to the sky.

'Benjamin! I salute you. Watch over me, Ben!'

Then he took Barbara's hand and they slewed their way by moonlight down the lanes towards the water.

'You don't like the sea, and I don't like it either, any more,' Will said. 'But we won't go there, and we won't go on the path. We'll just go to the shed.'

'What shed?' Barbara said. 'There isn't a shed.'

'I wanted to live there when I was younger. My Huckleberry Finn shed.'

The land was sold now and the boats were gone, but the shed remained. A nail still kept the hasp in place, and when they opened the door, they found it still full of gear.

'Will?' Barbara's voice was anxious. 'Are you sure?'

But he was. It was just where he wanted to be, and he took her hand and pulled her in.

'There are rugs and a groundsheet in here somewhere,' he said. 'No electric now, but there are candles too, don't ask me why.'

He held his lighter up in the dark, the whoozy flame making things jump, till they found the candles. Then spread the groundsheet, and the rugs over. Will felt more sober, and he took a swig from the bottle they'd brought with them. He looked at Barbara. She had taken off her shoes when they left the road – 'I'll kill myself in those heels' – wincing her way over the cold ground in her stockinged feet. Now she sat in the middle of the rug and took off the stockings, unfastening the clips from her garter belt.

'Don't watch,' she said, her voice still a little drunk.

Her hair, piled high for the party, was beginning to tumble.

'Looks like seaweed,' Will said, lifting it and letting it drop.

When she was done with the stockings, she wrapped her arms around herself.

'We should climb under,' he said. 'Stay warm.'

Barbara's brown eyes seemed black in the candlelight, and as she moved, her body moved in and out of the shadows.

Awkwardly they held one another, and kissed, gently at first and then harder. Will kissed her girl's face and shut his eyes.

He would have come here with Ben, he would have wrapped him up in these rugs and surrounded him with candles.

Will pressed himself against her softer body and he felt her fingers on his belt, under his shirt, on his fly, daring to touch him, daring him.

He would have kissed Benjamin, hard on the lips, in the mouth; would have kissed his nipples, would have bitten his ear, his neck.

He ran his hand down her skirt, down to the hem. He stroked her legs.

He said: 'I'm a stranger here. If you can help.'

AIR

On the ceiling, the little yellow stars glowed brighter. He'd get drunk tonight, and tomorrow he would bury his father. Will let his head sink into the cool pillow. It was half way to dark in here and if he wasn't careful, he would fall asleep. He glanced about, and from round the edges of the room Cassie's toys and piles of stuff seemed to watch him back: pop stars stared from magazines and dolls made glassy eyes at him. It smelt different in here to the rest of the flat, fresher, less used, and he felt his old familiar ache.

Will wondered what his father had known in that final, reduced month of his life. Last week he had sat by his bed on the plastic hospital chair and seen how little space his father took up now – just a crumpled shape beneath the sheets – and he'd held his father's hand. It wasn't such an old hand, because his father wasn't such an old man. But it had been heavy, and so still, not the faintest twitch of a finger, as if it were no longer inhabited. He'd looked at the veins like raised roots, the liver spots, the filigree of grey hairs that ran down each finger. And he'd noticed that the fingernails were getting long, and hunted for clippers in the bedside cupboard, because his father always kept them neat. Finding none, he'd slipped his father's hands beneath the covers.

He'd barely spoken to his father; they'd never talked much and it didn't occur to him to begin now, when George was dying. But curious, he had touched his cheek. It felt soft and yielding, as if it had given itself up to its own ghost. He'd never touched his father's face before. As he got up to leave, he'd noticed his father's watch, made safe and silent. Picking it up, he'd wound it and set the hands right, and strapped it gently onto his father's wrist. Then he'd bent over the bed and kissed his brow.

'Always a first time,' he'd said.

A strand of cobweb drifted to and fro in Cassie's window, and his thoughts drifted with it. He thought how hard it was, being a good father, especially now, now that Cassie was this age, and he fell into remembering, different scenes, different times, and before he could stop himself, the remembering took him somewhere else and he was over the edge, his stomach lurching, head over feet over mind.

They'd made such a good show of it at first. They were a beautiful couple, to themselves most of all. He went to university and Barbara found work in London. They spent time together: parties, films, weekends, trips home occasionally. They had sex. Though that was when it was hardest, when he most needed not to think; and he often wondered what it could be like for her. She seemed to enjoy it and he was always gentle, but really he didn't know, and he never asked. Asking would have been too risky. You got your fingers burnt for asking. And what about for him? For him, the sex was shadow play, pretending. He never longed for it. He never felt that insatiability, that hunger that he'd known for Ben. But they loved each other, and they made each other laugh; that was good enough.

It was late in the summer he finished university that he took the train to Devon on his own for the weekend. As he walked up from the village, there was a golden, early evening light that made everything look possible. Sitting high up on the gatepost, Emma was waiting for him, her dress pulled in between her legs for decorum. She was brown from a summer outside, and had her hair cut short. With her gangly, teenage shape, she still looked more of a boy than a girl, except for the dress.

'Mother thinks you're a bringer of tidings,' she said.

'I have a message from Barbara,' he said, 'Which is: "Max Factor. Strawberry meringue." That's word for word.'

Emma punched the air.

'She said you'd understand,' Will said.

She jumped down, brushed off her dress and took his arm, striding to match his steps. Her arm seemed so light in his, and he envied her, standing there, so jaunty, on the edge of growing up.

'Barbara's too good for you,' Emma said.

'Says who?'

Emma shrugged.

'They're right, whoever said it,' he said.

He found Meg, as ever, in the greenhouse. The air was rich and sweet. He sat, as he always had, in the old wicker chair and watched her swing the watering can. How often had he watched her like this? All his life, that he could remember.

He noticed, and this was for the first time, how measured, how slow her movements were, as if this – this tending to all that grew in here – were the only task she had in the world. The water flashed across beds of salad and cucumbers, and pots with tomatoes that shone like jewels. She had seen him, marked his presence with the slightest move of the head, and after a minute she spoke.

'I know why you're here,' she said. 'And she is a lovely girl.'

'Yes,' he said.

She tilted the can and he waited.

'As long as you're sure,' she said at last. 'As long as you don't find yourself wishing she was someone else. Something else.'

'I don't wish that,' he said. 'And I thought the news would make you glad.'

She put down the watering can.

'I am glad,' she said. 'I am.'

But there was something in her voice he didn't understand. He stood and walked over to her and when she turned, he saw that she was crying.

'Mother?' he said.

He felt a little boy again, to find her crying for something that he didn't know about or understand.

'Pay no attention,' she said, and she wiped away her tears. Then: 'I only worry that you are too like me,' she said.

'And that's a bad thing?'

'Sometimes one should act in spite of the world and his wife,' and she smiled and put a hand to his hair, smoothed it with her fingers.

'But if you're sure, then I am glad for both of you,' she said. 'So go and find your father,' she said. 'You'll make him proud.'

The next years were tumbled in Will's mind like broken china: fragments with a snatch of colour or a half-design, though their sharp edges were smoother now. A life in London, work, marriage, friends, busyness. Days filled up, kept busy, so there was no time for being sad. It was true that he could still be caught by surprise: by the glance of light off the fountain water in Trafalgar Square, or a stray gull's cry high above the streets, or the stretch of sky before him as he walked on a city heath. Without thinking, he'd put his fingers to his collar-bone and feel the scar scorched on there. It was a medallion, the measure of something; and he'd go on with a sense of sadness he wouldn't name, but which he couldn't, for a while, put away. Once he went with three friends, three other husbands, on a summer trip. They camped beside the River Wye and fished for salmon. The river was gorgeous, and the mood in the group was easy, relaxed. But Will didn't enjoy it. It brought things too close and it was harder to be himself, sleeping close to the other men, and with the water, and the dying fish, and he turned the offer down when it came again.

The morning Cassie was born, the day was still so new, so early, that it seemed to Will he had the whole world to himself. His baby, his new baby girl, had been born in the small hours and now she filled up his mind's eye. He'd left her sleeping in her sleeping mother's arms and come out, euphoric, into a city that was still, incredibly, asleep. Once already he'd crossed the river and not even noticed, running over Westminster Bridge as if he could take flight above the dozy pigeons, above the sleeping boats. He ran and ran and he saw only her dark, wet hair, her perfect ears, her fists like walnuts, her puckered mouth. Past Embankment tube station and up the steps, still running, and on to the grimy stretch of Hungerford Bridge, his spirits exhilarated, boundless.

Still he saw nothing except his baby's perfect face and he ran on, coat tails flapping, until, halfway across, fatigue struck. His legs turned to lead, his lungs burned in his chest, and he was forced to a halt. Chest heaving, eyes blurred, he walked over to the rail; leaned on it, looked down. The sky was dawning grey, and the river was grey beneath, gagging and churning. Behind him, a train rumbled by. Between the air and the water Will stood and perhaps it was so much space, or it was the running; or perhaps it was hunger, because he hadn't eaten much in the last twelve hours; or perhaps it was the new life he was responsible for, he didn't know. But something overwhelmed him – dizziness, vertigo, terror – and he felt himself pulled beyond the edge, pulled into his fear, into the air, till he was reaching over and clinging on, staring down at the dirty Thames, repulsed and longing.

'Hey, mate.'

There was a hand on his shoulder, and he started.

'You all right?'

He was confused. His head felt blood-rushed and his fingers were fizzy and numb. He nodded, or he thought he did, and made to stand upright.

'I'll give you a hand,' the voice said. 'You look a bit ropey.'

He sounded young and male, and rough with something. Will felt his elbows grasped, then he was half-pulled, half-lifted away from the edge, and a hand steadied him on his feet.

'There,' the voice said.

Will turned. He was very young, more boy than man, and dressed in dirty jeans and an old anorak. He wore a battered rucksack with a bedroll slung below.

'Thanks,' Will said. 'Got out of breath, dizzy.'

'It's fine,' the boy said. 'Sure.'

'Could do with a cup of tea,' Will said. He was cold, still shaky. He needed to sit down. 'Anywhere round here you know of?' because it was still very early, too early for most places.

'There's a place off The Cut'll be open by now,' the boy said.

He bought the boy a cup of tea and a full English, and watched him eat it in double quick time, eyes glancing up with every mouthful as if someone might take it off him. They didn't talk. The boy was sleeping rough, but he had an appetite and Will thought that must be a good thing. Afterwards, as if they had discussed it, as if it were already understood, the boy took Will to a quiet alley, and Will fucked him.

He never told Barbara. Of course he didn't, and anyway, he'd sworn it wouldn't happen again. He had stood beside the hospital bed and looked down at his wife still sleeping, at his daughter, and sworn it. It was just because of the day it was, he told himself. His mind, his emotions out of kilter.

But he was wrong about that.

In that first year of Cassie's life he marvelled at her single-mindedness, her sheer tenacity as she learned to crawl, and stand, and walk, and say 'Dada' and then 'Mama', and hold tiny things in her fingers. He marvelled at all the hard work there was in being a baby, and he clapped and cheered her, his gorgeous, round-faced diva daughter. But while Cassie thrived, his marriage died. The boy on the bridge had unlocked something in him, and soon he was living a second life that had its geography mapped out in secret places and borrowed times. Lunch hours, after work, sometimes even late at night he cruised. The sex was like a drug, each fix assuaging something for a time until the hunger came again. He told himself it did no damage. That the cruising was in one place, and his family in another. He told himself he loved his wife more fiercely for it. He told himself he could stop at any point. And he didn't think about Benjamin; wouldn't let himself. But when Barbara found him out and said to him: 'Don't lie to me,' he wept, because it was the end between them.

Eventually he built a safe life for himself; an ordered, functioning life. He lived alone, he did his job, he had his friends, he saw his daughter and sometimes he cruised for sex. But each within its bounds. He was careful and he didn't let things overlap. As the years built and Barbara remarried, Meg would ask him sometimes if there was anyone else in the picture, a woman perhaps. And sometimes he would make somebody up, a Catherine or an Alison, and take them on imaginary dates; but mostly he would say that Cassie was the only girl for him.

Gradually Will's head steadied. He knew what to do when things fell away; how to sit up slowly and make himself breathe, deep breaths in, and slow out, and haul himself back from the edge. Then stand, though his legs were like lead, and find the solid land. He had learned how to go out of the room and shut the door behind him again, and he did that now. But he still wondered where his father was. The father he would bury tomorrow. Because in all Will's tumbling thoughts, he had been nowhere.

The day had gone to dark while he lay remembering. He stared at the windows in the flat. Outside it rained but he saw nothing but himself reflected back. His father was a man who believed that things were as they seemed. That clocks told the passage of time, and that clothes told the man. When Ben died, his father had sold the land he died on and the boat he died carrying, as if it were those things that had failed him, and not Will, and not Ben's own bolt-struck heart.

Will went into the kitchen and cut the electricity to the green digits of the oven clock, then took out the batteries from the clock beside the bed. In the bathroom he turned the metal key against the grain, felt the cogs protest. He pulled out the winder on his watch so the hands were held just there. And last of all, he went into the sitting room.

He loved this room, its different geometries, its different objects: the long, angular sofas, the zig-zag pattern on the grey rug runner, the tall, white blinds in the tall windows. In place of the hearth there was the stainless steel cylinder of a Pither stove, and on the walls he had mounted a series of African masks, their features flattened and elongated. Only one thing in here seemed anomalous. It was an eighteenth-century bracket clock that stood on four carved feet in a mahogany casing on the side table, and it had been a gift from his parents on his twenty-first birthday. Every seventh day Will wound it and in two minutes it would strike out the hour. But now he opened the case and stilled the pendulum with a soft hand.

'No more time, Father,' he said.

Then he got newspaper, tugging it urgently from the pile, and grabbed a whisky tumbler and the new bottle of Johnnie Walker, took them into the sitting room. He spread the newspaper over the floor, and fetched his shoes, half a dozen pairs, and the shoe-cleaning box from the bedroom. They were hand-stitched brogues and Oxfords; shoes his father approved of. Opening the bottle, he poured himself a glass and drank it straight down. He didn't like whisky very much, but tonight it was what he needed and he poured a second.

George had given him this box years ago when Will got his first proper job. It was polished with brass hinges and a brass plate engraved with his name: William Garrowby. Inside were brushes, a shoehorn, soft cloths and tins of polish – tan, black, brown – each in its apportioned place.

'Always look at a man's shoes if you want to know what you're dealing with,' George had said. 'It's a good rule of thumb. And when you're cleaning, watch out for the seams and the crevices; that's where the dirt gets in.'

Then George had poured them each a Johnnie Walker and lifted his glass to Will's success.

Time and shiny shoes: his father's bequest. Will ran his finger over his name and picked up the first shoe. Remembering calmed him and with his father's voice in his mind, he cleaned as George had taught him, brushing in the polish, taking care with the eyeholes, and using a soft cloth to buff a deeper colour into the heel and the toe. Sometimes his tears dropped on to the leather uppers and he rubbed them in too. He cleaned and buffed till every shoe shone, and till he had drunk four fingers of the whisky. Then he put the shoes away and stood up. He was stiff from kneeling for so long and he felt heavy with sadness, or anger, or loneliness, he didn't know which.

'Clean shoes, Father,' he said, and he laughed. 'Fuck it. I never got it right.'

The funeral director gave each of them black gloves to wear. Pallbearers' gloves.

'They're one-size,' he said, which was for Emma who was the only woman. They were flimsy, cotton things and Will didn't think they'd be proof against anything much. The funeral director told them to double-tie their shoelaces and to be careful where they put their feet because the aisle was uneven. They were to set the coffin down on the trolley at the front, then take their seats until the very end, when they would carry the coffin out again. Emma had the middle position on the left, behind him, and Henry was on the right. As they lifted the coffin to their shoulders, he heard Emma gasp; just a small sound, maybe no more than an intake of breath as she shouldered her father. Slowly, carefully, they walked into the church. It was full and as he walked down the aisle, he felt the movement, like a soft wave, as people turned to watch. Head against the coffin he pictured his father, lying just the other side of the varnished wood, his brow close to Will's, resting on its quilted pillow. Nearly close enough to kiss.

He thought: You didn't know very much about me, and now you've died, so that's that.

For the rest of the service Will stood outside of things, as if he'd drifted some way off. He rose and sat at the correct times, and sang the hymns: 'Fight the good fight', he sang, and 'Rock of ages, cleft for me'. He marked the course of the vicar's voice, rising and falling. He looked round at his mother, who was dressed in her own kind of serenity and who struck him as looking stoical and beautiful. There was Henry, and Barbara, and there was Emma. Emma held her pallbearers' gloves in one hand, her finger stroking and stroking the cheap black cotton. And beside him sat Cassie. She looked older than her twelve years, with her hair up and her sober dress. When he sat down, she took his hand.

'You all right?' he said.

'I can't believe he's in there, It's too weird.' She didn't cry, only kept tight hold.

When it was time for the eulogy, he took out his script, walked to the front, and spoke in a clear, steady voice. He captured George's strengths and his passions, and was affectionate about his oddities. He conjured up a man who had risen out of poverty to forge a life of prosperity and security; a man his wife, children, and friends, would all remember as enthusiastic, energetic, often exacting, and passionately fair. A man who kept his word, and kept the time (there was a kind laugh at that); who was a loving husband and father and a devoted friend.

He looked down at the front pew. Barbara was nodding and Henry was smiling as he spoke. His mother stared straight back at him, her chin lifted, her expression . . . he didn't know what her expression was. Proud, perhaps; or defiant. Emma had her arm around Cassie's shoulder and each of them was crying. He thought: at last I've got it right. First time ever. Bang on, and he's not bloody here to see it. And he thought that if it were him in that long box, being cried for, then nobody would get it right.

Things were nearly over when Meg put her hand on his arm. People had eaten and drunk, and talked his father deep into the ground and most of them had left now. Barbara had gone to see her parents in the village. In the sitting room Cassie played Monopoly with Emma and Henry. Will went to find her, breathe her in as he used to when she was a baby. She had found from somewhere his old sailing cap, and when he kissed the top of her head, he could still smell the sea in it. He watched them for a minute, till he felt his mother's hand.

'Will,' she said, nothing more, but he heard the appeal in her voice so he turned and followed her out.

They sat on the old bench in the garden, out of sight of the house. She looked very pale, and he wondered if perhaps she was falling ill.

'I have to tell you something. Now George has died,' she said.

She paused and he saw how her hands clutched and unclutched.

'Is everything all right?' he said. 'I mean beyond . . .' and he made a gesture that took in their funeral clothes, the death between them.

She didn't reply immediately. Her hands were fists on her lap, and when she did speak, she looked ahead of her, to the drop in the sky where the sea began.

'This is very hard,' she said, her voice so quiet, it was as though she were speaking to someone else.

'Mother?' he said, because her breath was coming quickly now and she was biting her lip and still staring ahead, and he worried that she was ill; or that her mind had become over-strained in these last weeks.

'Perhaps you could leave it till later,' he said. 'Till tomorrow. I'll be here tomorrow. Or we could talk next time . . .'

'No!' She said it so fiercely, then more quietly: 'No, now. You spoke about him well in the church. He would have been proud. And he was a good man.'

'Yes,' Will said.

'We had a long marriage, and he was a good man . . .' she said again, as though she needed to impress this upon herself.

Will rubbed at his face. He felt bleary, as if he'd just woken.

Questions blundered through his head: Had his father done something wrong? Was it the will? Or debts? Did he have a mistress?

'And you have to speak to me first?' he said, looking round at her. 'Before Henry or Emma?'

'Yes.'

She had always told her children to look at the person they were speaking to, and she always did so herself. But she didn't – wouldn't – meet Will's eye now. Finally she continued.

'You remember the story I used to tell about how I went to Africa in the war, to marry your father.' It wasn't a question, and Will waited. 'I used to tell you about the ship, and how it was torpedoed, and the lifeboat, and George waiting for me. And how we got married immediately.'

'Of course I do,' Will said.

It was one of his earliest memories: sitting at the big, shiny table, listening. He saw himself, elbows planted high, and the light coming in through the windows, and the pale blue plate in front of him. His mother still had some of that china.

'Everything I told you was true,' Meg said. But she shut her eyes a moment and shook her head.

'Mother?' he said.

'I can't do this,' she said. 'I don't know how to do this.'

Far off, near the house, there was the noise of a car on gravel, then voices, fading quickly.

'It's fine. I understand.' He was coming out with platitudes because he didn't know what else to say, but he couldn't bear seeing his mother like this. 'Leave it for now.'

She pushed his hand away.

'No. It has to be today,' and like someone jumping into icy water, she took a deep breath, shut her eyes, and went on.

'I did something. Only once. It just happened the once, but . . .'

Will waited, shifting on the bench, which was narrow, and too low for him to be comfortable.

'I was very young, travelling on that ship, and very lost. I can see that now.'

She spoke in quick, short bursts, as if the words were gathered under pressure.

'I knew I'd lost my brother, of course – though I'd never stopped searching. But I didn't know I'd lost myself too.'

Will had never heard his mother talk like this. Never. Not about anything, and he wanted her to stop, and he wanted her to carry on.

She caught her breath and then, abruptly, spoke in a rush as if to get it out quickly, before anything happened, before she couldn't bear to.

'I'm not trying to excuse myself. Because of you, I've never regretted what happened, not for a second. And I've never told anyone before. Not a single person.'

'Because of me?' Will said.

'I met a soldier. I was lost in the ship; very lost, and he rescued me.'

'A soldier?'

He'd have been in terrible trouble if he'd been caught . . . but he took me back to my cabin.'

'So?'

'He's your father, Will.'

Nothing happened. Nothing moved, or exploded, or dropped to the earth. Will stood up and walked off a little way. He wanted to laugh. That was his first feeling. That it was so funny. Far out, over where the sea was, the sky was black with a storm that might never arrive. But it had coloured up the late afternoon sun, and all the trees were blocked in, each in a different light, as if each stood in its own kingdom. He looked at his mother. Her face was like a mask, all emotion hidden behind.

'Is there any doubt?' he said.

She shook her head.

'And Father?'

'He never knew.'

He looked down at his shiny shoes.

'Are you sure of that?' he said.

Everything was quiet. The birds had gone silent, and the air was still, windless.

Then: 'You could have told me before the funeral. I feel like a fool. I stood up in the church today behind that shiny eagle as George Garrowby's eldest son, and I did it very well. I know I did; I could tell when I looked at everyone sitting there.'

The brewing storm had moved further off now, over the sea, and the sky had cleared to the palest blue.

'What was his name?' he said.

'Jim,' she said. 'Jim Cooper.'

Then she said: 'I'm sorry.'

Anger flashed through him, electric, convulsive.

'So you had your soldier on the ship, and then Father a few weeks later.'

He might as well have hit her; he saw her start, then square herself as if to acknowledge the blow.

'It wasn't like that,' she said, but he didn't want to know.

'Ring on your finger, done and dusted. So easy,' he said, and his words were stones, pelted one after the other. 'Why did you have to tell me?'

He twisted away and put his hands to his head, as if he could shake her out. His ears were buzzing and he felt the headrush of vertigo.

'He always loved Henry more than me. Right from the start, even in Africa. But it's no wonder, is it?'

'He loved you, Will. He was proud of you.'

'And he couldn't have borne it, could he? Knowing, I mean. His bastard son. He had to have everything respectable. In its proper bloody place . . .'

'Stop it,' she said.

' . . . shined up nicely. Because that's what he cared most about.'

'Stop it, Will.'

Her voice was cold and when he turned, her fists were raised, as if she might hit him; as if she might rain down blows with her fists in a pantomime rage. But slowly she lowered them.

'How dare you? We buried him today.'

And he watched her walk back up the garden and out of sight.

Maybe it was a long time, or maybe it wasn't very long that

he sat there for, he didn't know. But it was long enough for the sun to drop below the tree line and for his mind to settle. He was still angry – how could he not be? – but now mixed in with his anger was something else, something more difficult to name.

He found his mother where he'd hoped to. The greenhouse door was shut, but he could see her in there, head down, intent at something. He watched her. She must have come straight here from the garden; she wore an old tweed jacket of his father's over her mourning dress, the cuffs bundled roughly, and as she worked, they dipped in the soil. Will shivered and rubbed his arms. He was cold. He opened the greenhouse door. It was warm inside with the steamy fragrant warmth of so many plants, so much green.

Briefly she looked up. He saw that she'd been crying, and wondered who it was for. For him? Or his father? For herself? He spoke to her profile.

'I'm sorry for what I said earlier. About Father.'

She nodded slightly.

'Well, it's done now,' she said, though he couldn't tell whether she said it about his words, or hers. But he saw something relax in her face, and so he sat down in the old wicker chair.

'And the soldier,' he said. 'I had rather know than not know.'

'Yes.' Gently she took a plant from its pot, seeming to cradle the mess of roots in her hand. 'I know that,' she said. 'I do know that.'

'But do you know the strangest thing, Mother? The strangest thing is that already I'm not so surprised.'

He watched her fill round the roots, pressing the soil firm with her fingers. She was so gentle and he remembered how she used to put her hand to his head sometimes, stroke his hair to reassure. He looked away, stared at all the green. There was something on his mind that was hard to broach. His mouth was very dry and he licked his lips.

'Here.' Meg handed him a small lemonade bottle. 'But careful,' she said, as he tipped it up. A blast of alcohol lanced his throat.

'You don't like whisky,' he said.

She gave a small smile.

'George didn't like me drinking it. Not a female drink. So I've always kept it in here.'

The whisky warmed him; he felt its Dutch courage. He watched his mother with her plants. Her hands were busy but she was waiting. He could see it in her.

'Do you remember what you told me the day Benjamin died?' he said.

The question had come unbidden. It had come from deep inside, forming as it rose and when he spoke it, it took him by surprise as much as his mother. She didn't reply immediately. Just carried on with her plants. Will uncrossed his arms and laid his hands on the chair arms, as if an easier position might give him an easier spirit. The chair wicker was brittle under his fingers and he caught at a piece, lifted it till it snapped. Placing it in his palm, he closed his fist around it till the sharp ends pressed into his skin. Then he waited, as he had waited when he was a boy, for his mother to help him out here.

'I told you a lot of things then,' Meg said at last. 'Too many, perhaps.'

'But you do know what I'm talking about, don't you?'

'I told you to live your own life.'

But he pressed her, because he had to now. 'And you knew, didn't you? You knew what he was to me.'

She spoke slowly then, and carefully. 'You've kept your secret very close all these years, just as I have mine,' and he saw her flinch at her own words.

'Too close?'

'I don't know. But I do know that I was frightened to do otherwise. Don't make the same mistake. You're a father as well as a son, Will. You need to think about Cassie.'

Cassie ran along the field full-tilt. Her hair was loose from its clips, streaming out behind her. Behind her, Will came more slowly. As he walked, he pulled off his tie, coiled it round his fingers and put it in his pocket, and he opened the neck of his shirt. At the end of the field the woods began and the path dipped deep between the trees to the beach. Down here tree roots lurched across so you had to watch your footing, and branches reached down to clip the unsuspecting. When Cassie was little, Will used to carry her. He'd tell her stories of serpents rearing up, and twig sprites that might dandle their fingers in her hair, and she'd clutch his shoulders harder with her small hands and bury her face in his neck.

By the time Will reached the trees, Cassie was out of sight and he walked down the path on his own till he came to the beach.

The sea was calm and smooth, and the sun was low by now, throwing long shadows where it could. On the far side, some children still played in the stream, building castles, spading the water into tributaries, organising against the tide. He looked out to the thin lip of horizon, and back for his daughter. In the middle of the empty beach, Cassie stood with her arms out. She whirled them up and round, making a windmill, and stood still again. She looked happy there and then, not a care in the world.

'Perhaps I should leave it for today,' he said to himself. 'Enough gone on already.'

He walked over the sand, passing the little heap of shoes and socks she had left. Now she ran, kicking up the sand, flinging her arms and legs around her, and her shadow flung itself even further. He thought how she was still a girl, and nearly not.

'Dad!' she yelled out. 'The sand's warm. Take your shoes off.'

He shook his head.

'Come on,' Cassie called. 'Just this once.'

'I'm fine as I am,' he called back, and she shrugged and turned away.

Will crouched and laid his hands on the sand. He dug his fingers in and through, down to the knuckles, down to the cold. He wanted nothing better than to play on this beach for an hour with his daughter. He wanted to fling his shadow about like her, and watch her dance. He looked around. She was crouched down now making a desultory castle. He punched the sand hard. The impact jarred through his arm, into his shoulder. He punched again. All those years, all that time, his visits as a young man, then married, a father, divorced: all that time Meg had known about Benjamin. Perhaps she knew why he split up with Barbara. Perhaps she guessed why he'd never met another girlfriend.

He picked up a small stone, placed it in his palm. It was smooth and flat, edges worn by the sea. Once it would have been part of the slate rocks that sliced either side of the beach. But it had probably been tumbled in the tides for years, and now here it was, adrift on the sand in its own shadow. He made a fist around it, clenching to make it hurt. Slipping the stone into his jacket pocket, he looked around for another, and another, and when his pockets were full, he walked back towards his daughter.

He'd built his life around a secret. Sworn Barbara to silence, kept it from his child, pretended to something else. He shook his head. This was stupid. He was so fucking stupid. Something blew across his mind – an image, a memory perhaps: a man and a boy, bundled up against the cold, walking together, no more than that, and he wondered who his father *was*. He'd felt so angry with his mother, but now he just felt sad. All his life she'd kept his father secret from him, and it struck him that she had held her memory – her love, and her sadness – as closely, as jealously to her as he had held his. And he wondered what it had cost her, to keep her secret all these years. If it had cost her as much as it had cost him.

He had learned, as a boy, to skim a stone a long way; and in that boy way, he could have still told you the method of it, if he thought you might hear him out. Because if you hold a stone flat between thumb and first two fingers, draw your arm back behind you, keeping it parallel with the beach, then fling your arm forward, only making sure to flick the stone with your wrist and spin it at the last with your index finger, the stone will fly. It will kiss-kiss-kiss the surface of the sea, in unlikely, ineffable flight, seeming to defy both its own stony gravitas, and the sea's, before dropping beneath. Sometimes, of course, you will pitch it badly, or it will catch a stony edge and sink immediately. Or the sea will be too choppy and unreliable to skim upon. But sometimes, if the sea is smooth and the stones are good, then they will walk on the water for you.

Rummaging in his pocket, he took out the stones and skimmed the first, throwing it as hard as he could against the surface of the sea, and counted it out till the sea took it in. He breathed and the air was salt and light. He thought about George, and their leave-taking. He skimmed a second stone, and just for a moment he remembered Ben, sleeping like a dancer. He skimmed a third. Each looked as if it would fly forever, and was gone.

Cassie came and stood beside him, out of breath and sandy-footed.

'You want one?' he said, and she gave him a look, as if to say: there's a whole beach of them, but she held out her hand.

Side by side they threw stones at the sea, and his danced and hers sank.

'Show me,' she said, so they collected some more and she watched.

'Bend so you're nearer to the water,' he said, 'and make it spin with your finger.'

She threw again.

'Do you miss Grandfather?' she said.

The sea was sheer like grey silk, and imperturbable.

'Yes,' Will said. 'I do.'

'It was peaceful, wasn't it? His death, I mean.'

'Yes, it was peaceful.'

'I don't think I do miss him yet,' she said. 'Him being dead — it's too new still. But next time I'm down here, then I will.'

And Will thought that she was more truthful than him. Because what he missed was a man he never knew. He pictured the two of them, father and child, as tiny figures caught between these planes of sky and land and sea.

'Cassie?' he said. 'I need to tell you a story. About me, and your mother,' and she rolled her eyes and groaned.

But she said: 'Go on then. Tell me.'

So he did. He told her about Benjamin, his closest friend. About their perfect day, and about how Ben had died.

She didn't move while he spoke, or say a word. But when he stopped, she walked to the water's edge and he watched her stretch out her arm and take aim, closing one eye to line up her sight, pull her arm back and throw. She was trying to make the stone jump, but she was awkward, all elbows, and her stone didn't bounce. She threw again and the stone sank again. Then she turned to Will.

'So what?' she said. 'You, and your friend, and all of it. What's any of it got to do with Mum? Or me?'

He took a breath, because this was it, this was the shadow. The thing he had to say. And he spoke again.

'This is the story, Cassie. The reason it didn't work out with your mother; the reason I'm not married. It's because I'm gay. I was in love with Ben, with the boy who died. That's who I really am, and I should have explained it before . . .' He paused. 'Cassie?' he said.

But she had turned away. Now she threw anything, anyhow. She stood at the water's edge and threw stones that had no chance of flight. Will stood at her back, his arms heavy at his sides. He wanted to leave; walk briskly up between the trees and get in the car, go back to the house, have a drink.

He thought: I shouldn't have told her. I shouldn't have said anything.

Cassie didn't stop until she had thrown every stone around her, slinging and hurling and hefting them. Gently, smoothly, the sea came in, the gentle waves darkening her jeans. Will watched and waited. He wished he knew his daughter better. When she turned he saw anger in her face, and hurt.

'Show me how,' she said.

So standing behind her, he covered her arm with his, her hand with his.

'Like this,' he said.

Then he gave her a stone from his pocket and stood away a

little. She threw it and it skimmed the sea once, twice, a third and a fourth time.

'See?' she said, turning to him.

And she took another stone from him and threw.

ACKNOWLEDGEMENTS

Thanks to Mrs Drue Heinz and the Trustees of Hawthornden Castle for the residency during which a portion of this novel was written. Thanks also to the Royal Literary Fund and its Writing Fellowship scheme which has provided me with gainful employment and enabled me to continue writing.

Chris Holme gave me invaluable advice about electricity and voltage, but any mistakes made are mine alone. And David Attwell and John Greening provided useful advice and suggestions about African literature.

My thanks to John Baker, Karen Charlesworth, Frances Coad, Sarah Edington, Sandy Goldbeck-Wood, Anthea Gomez, Liz Grierson, Eliza Haughton-Shaw, Jesse Haughton-Shaw, Nicky Losseff, Sophie Mayer, Sara Perrin and Martin Riley for much and various support, inspiration and storytelling.

Many thanks also to Sam Humphreys for excellent and patient editing; and to Rebecca Gray and all at Serpent's Tail.

And finally my thanks to Clare Alexander, from first to last a wonderful agent.